Broken Soldier

Lost Hearts Novella

Blue Saffire

Perceptive Illusions Publishing, Inc.
Bay Shore, New York

Blue Saffire/Perceptive Illusions Publishing, Inc.
23 Chris Matt Ct.
Bay Shore, New York 11706
www.BlueSaffire.com

Publisher's Note: This is a work of fiction. Names, characters, places, and incidents are a product of the author's imagination. Locales and public names are sometimes used for atmospheric purposes. Any resemblance to actual people, living or dead, or to businesses, companies, events, institutions, or locales is completely coincidental.

Ordering Information:
Quantity sales. Special discounts are available on quantity purchases by corporations, associations, and others. For details, contact the "Special Sales Department" at the address above.

Broken Soldier: Lost Hearts Series Novella/ Blue Saffire. – 2nd ed.
ISBN 978-1-941924-66-2

The lost and broken will find their way.

−Blue Saffire

Survivor

Parker

I can hardly see a thing. My NVGs shattered in the last explosion. I have so much adrenaline pumping through me. I feel like I'm moving on autopilot. This isn't my first rodeo, but this is a bad one.

I can't believe I'm still here.

I can feel the loss of my brothers as if we're connected at the soul. I can't think about that now. I have to keep moving. I push all feelings to the back of my mind, including the searing pain on my entire left side.

I fire through my blurry vision, before trying to search around me once again. My best friend, my brother in arms, the man I trust with my life was just with me. He'd taken a hit to the leg, but I had him.

"Myles," I bellow out, as gunfire continues to erupt around me.

My earpiece is useless. Nothing is coming through. I can't hear shit from my team. The ringing in my ears from the blast has finally subsided. I squint to look around again.

"Redding!"

My blood runs cold, when he doesn't respond. I can hear the moans and groans of others, but something in my bones tells me that none of those belong to Myles. I focus, allowing my ears to guide me. I begin to count.

One, two...three...four, five...six, seven, eight. Fuck.

I make out nine. I can hear the gunfire of my men. We started as twelve. I listen and count again, hoping my ears are deceiving me. My chest tightens when confirmation greets my eardrums like a ringing bell.

The loudest silence is the silence closest to me. Myles, I don't hear close enough fire to say he's okay. My team members are spread out, but none that are firing are close enough for me to rest in the fact that my closest brother is still with me.

Suddenly, the hairs stand up on the back of my neck as an ear-splitting whistle pierces the air. I know it's coming, death has breathed his breath through the air. I'll be lucky if I don't inhale this time.

CHAPTER ONE

Broken Soldier

Parker

Every fucking inch of my body hurts. My lids feel like weights have been placed on them, my left side feels like it's on fire in some places and completely numb in others. Yet, I know I'm alive. I don't know if I can say the same for my unit. I don't know if I can say the same for Myles.

Myles and I moved up the ranks together. It was a no brainer to enter the Special Forces knowing he would be on my team. Myles was there when I found out my fiancée was leaving me for some real estate douche bag she'd been fucking for years. I still remember the words he whispered in my ear to keep me from losing my shit.

"Fuck her, you'll have two more before the night is over. Let her have that sorry motherfucker and move on."

The words are so fresh in my mind, just like yesterday. Yet, I know it wasn't yesterday. It was two years ago. I'd like to say I got over it, but I never truly moved on. I knew I planned to stick around in the military for a few more years so I never bothered with a real relationship.

I was saving that for one hundred and twenty days from now. Six more months and Myles and I were going to retire. We both felt it in our bones that it was time. Ninety days and we were on our way to take leave. At least, it was ninety days when we rolled out, headed for camp in Herat. Afghanistan showed us it's fucking ass.

I grit my teeth in my dry mouth. I haven't opened my eyes because I'm not ready to face what's coming. The sound of the machines around me tell me I'm a survivor. I just don't know how many others are. Something tells me I'm not in hostile territory. I'm not getting that itch.

Suck it up, Parker. You have your life. Stop being a bitch.

I grunt, knowing the voice in my head has told no lie. Although in a motherfucking lot of pain, I'm breathing. I'll never take that for granted. Not like I once did, when I was young and dumb.

Believe it or not, I think Myles' sister is the reason I grew up. I've never met her in person, but I sure do feel like I know Myles' family as if they were my own. I've met them through stories, skype, and photographs. For some reason, I've never made it to Dallas, where Myles and his family are from.

I'm a Tennessee boy myself. Until last year, I had my daddy's ranch to go home to. When my father died, I sold the ranch and put away the money. Too many memories on that land for me. Also, not enough people I trust to take care of the place while I'm active duty.

Myles almost lost it when his baby sister, Lakia, broke the news to him that she'd gotten pregnant. It changed everything. Myles was so angry. Apparently, he never liked the fucker that knocked her up.

Myles wanted to go back home and murder the son of a bitch. I would've gone with him if his mama hadn't talked him off the ledge. Seeing the pictures of that little baby boy when he was born pulled something in my heart. I knew I had to be around to have his uncle's six. It was my job to always get Myles back to him.

For four years, I've done my fucking job. Now, I have this feeling in my gut that tells me I fucked up. I don't want to listen to the voices whispering that my best friend is no longer on this earth. It's just not something I can stomach.

"Promise me this, Parker. If I don't make it out of this desert, you'll take your ass to Texas as soon as you can and make sure my sister is alright. I'm so proud of her. She's doing her thing, but that bitch ass baby father of hers," he paused to shake his head. *"That motherfucker is going to make me put a bullet in his head.*

"If I'm not there to do it, I need it to be you. Promise," Myles demanded while locking those cola colored eyes on me.

"I'll make the promise, but it's not one I'll have to keep," I grinned at him.

I feel like a hole is blown through my chest as that memory surfaces. My eyes fly open. I have to get to Texas. I need to get to Lakia and Isaac. First thing I notice when I open my eyes, I can see, but I feel like I have tunnel vision. I blink a few times and still, nothing in my peripheral vision is clear.

I close my eyes, knowing that my SOF career is over. If I can't see, I can't be a part of the Special Forces. I'm done. Just one more loss, in a sea of more to come.

CHAPTER TWO

Loss

Lakia

It's been a long day of edits and revisions. I have a new book coming out next month. So much on my plate along with it. I just want to get into my mama's house for some of her smothered chicken and rice and peas.

That's the benefits of growing up in the Redding home. My mama's mix of West Indian roots and her Southern background are so good for the soul and the belly. She kept me eating good while pregnant with Isaac. It's no wonder that little boy scoffs down anything she places in front of him.

I love my son to pieces and back again. He's the reason I work so hard. I used to write a book a year and worked at the local college full-time. Once I got pregnant and had to stay off my feet, I started to write more and things just took off.

Funny how life can change in the blink of an eye. Toni has been the worst father in the world to my little guy, not to mention he has been a complete asshole to me. As much as I loathe him, I wouldn't change having my son for the world. Not even if it means washing away that look of disappointment my big brother gave me when he returned home to my swollen belly.

Myles is a great big brother. He talked me through my bad times. I know he was disappointed, but he has never ever made me feel like he has thought less of me. He has been nothing but supportive.

I smile at the thought of my big brother. He'll be home for good in just six months. Isaac thinks the world of him and has been counting down the days.

I turn the corner into my mama's block and my veins run cold. I feel like my body is suddenly covered in dry ice. Mama's house is at the head of the cul de sac, but even from here, I can see her crumbling in the doorway. I step on the gas, not even thinking. My car hops the small curb as I pull into her driveway.

I leap from the car while it's still running. I move right past the Chaplain. I don't need to hear what he's come to say. I already know.

"My baby," my mama's sobs loud enough to shake my soul.

I sink to my knees and wrap Mama in my arms. Myles was her everything, he could do no wrong. She'd been so relieved when he told her he was retiring. I know she was secretly counting down the days herself, while praying for his safe return.

"He promised he'd make it home," she continues. "This can't be. It just can't be. It's not his time. I know it's not his time."

My heart is breaking. It's breaking for my mama, it's breaking for my son, and it's breaking for me. My big brother could hang the moon. He was my protector, my voice of reason. The man I wanted my little boy to grow up looking up to.

CHAPTER THREE

Nice to Meet You

Parker

A month and a half later…

This has been the longest forty-four days in my life. I spent nine days in the hospital in Germany, before being sent to Brooke Army Medical in Texas. They kept me for another twenty-five days on account of my head being more fucked up than it already was.

Just as I knew, my career is done. I have moments of memory loss and at any given time, I lose my peripheral vision. I feel like a fucking horse with blinders. My left leg was burned pretty badly. Even after the skin grafting, so much nerve damage was done, I probably will never move or run the same.

Fuck, I'd live with all that shit happily if Redding, Cooper, and Graves were still here. We lost damn good men out there. I lost family. My soldiers were a part of me. I still can't believe Myles is gone.

The only thing that has made it feel real is the nagging feeling inside to get to Texas to his family. Myles words haven't stopped ringing in my ears. I need to be around for his baby sister and his nephew. Forty-four days has been too fucking long.

I haven't slept since I got on the plane from the base in North Carolina. I'd been there for ten days, itching to get my ass back here to Texas. It was the hardest thing in my life, knowing I was so close to Lakia and Isaac, but unable to go protect them the way my friend asked me to.

I'm here now. Hell, I couldn't be prouder of her. I've been standing in this line for four damn hours with giggling, babbling men and women, clamoring to get into the bookstore for their signed copies of Lakia's latest book.

I'm so damn proud. I can't say that enough. Myles would like to see this shit. I could see him now with his chest puffed out. I swallow hard as I think of him and what this would mean to him.

"You can move up, Honey," a voice says behind me.

I turn to see an older looking woman waving me forward. I turn back to see the line has moved ahead, leaving about three feet of empty space in front of me. At least I'm out of that hot ass sun. It wouldn't have bothered me much had it not been for the two complaining in front of me, for the last four hours.

Nodding, I close the gap, bringing the table stacked with books into view. In the center of those stacks sits the most gorgeous creature I've ever laid eyes on. Everything about her is stunning, from her dark chocolate skin to her long lashes that fan her cheeks while she looks down at the book she's signing.

I feel the breath leave my lungs when those lashes lift and her face turns up with the most beautiful smile on earth. She has Myles' cola colored eyes, hers are slanted just slightly more than his. Her lips are the most lush and full I've ever seen, but just right for her perfect heart shaped face.

That smile, it's lighting up the entire room. I look down to see I'm rubbing at my own chest. *Damn!* Myles wasn't a bad looking guy and I've seen Lakia on a skype or two in passing, but I never stopped to look and take her in. I mean, I've thought of her as a little sister all this time—the way Myles presented her to me.

Now, I wouldn't be a man if I didn't take note of the stunning woman sitting before me. Time seems to move without me. Soon I'm standing in front of the table and those eyes are staring right back at me.

I feel like I'm a kid again. I can't find my damn tongue to save my life. I feel like the geek I was before I went off to the military and bulked up. The teenager too shy to talk to girls at school. Not the confident soldier and known playboy I've become.

"Hi," she says softly, into the awkward silence.

Well, damn, damn, and damn again. Her voice is the sexiest thing I've ever heard. Soft, with a little rasp, but smooth like a well-loved whiskey. Fuck!

Lakia

He's gorgeous. Something about him is so familiar, but I would remember meeting a man as fine as him. That black hair, those piercing blue eyes. He is tall as fuck. He has to be six-five. His body is lean, but I can see the muscles rippling beneath his t-shirt and his thighs need to have mercy on those jeans.

Hot Damn!

He's the dirty, filthy, nasty shit my books are made of. The type of guy that dances in my head, as I write scene after scene. Those full pink lips—and Lawrt, help me—he has something slightly nerdy about him. Maybe it's the black glasses that are totally saying Clark Kent.

Yet, I know in my bones not to sleep on this man. I can feel the danger rolling off of him. It's the same feeling I used to have around my brother. That simple knowledge by staring at him, yes, this man as killed before.

"Hi," he says, shaking his head, seeming to try to clear it. "I'll take two please, if that's alright."

When I continue to sit and stare, he nods towards the books. I feel my cheeks burn, I drop my head, pulling my lip into my mouth. His fine ass has me feeling all types of stupid.

It's been so long since I've been a fool for a man. The last time it happened I ended up with a baby and a prick for a baby's father. Just thinking of Toni gives me the kick in the ass I need.

I reach for two copies of my latest book, not lifting my head to look at him again. My hand hovers over the page, when it dawns on me I didn't ask to who I'll be signing the book. He probably has some pretty girlfriend somewhere that he stood in line for.

That's sweet. Note to self. That needs to go in your next book.

"You can sign the first one to Parker," his southern drawl rumbles and I promise you I have to squeeze my thighs together.

Parker.

My brows pucker. Hearing that name in that sexy voice triggers something within. I feel a deep sadness, but still can't place where I may know this man from.

I shake it off and sign the book. My mind travels to my brother. The last month and a half has been one of the hardest times in my life. Losing my brother, then, my son's father suddenly wanting to come around more—and not at all because he wants to see his son.

This book signing was just the break I needed. I feel like I can't breathe at home. I have more deadlines coming, but it's been so hard. I'm so grateful to my girls. Kaye and Dean are my rocks. They've been writing as long as I have if not longer and neither are afraid to give me a good kick in the pants.

"Darlin', you can sign that second one to Redding. I know he'd be proud of you. I plan to take it to him," that rumbling drawl breaks into my thoughts.

My head pops up, my hand in mid-air. The gasp that leaves my lips takes all my breath with it. I narrow my eyes at the man I was ogling just minutes ago.

Parker.

"Oh, my God," I whisper. "Lieutenant Jake Parker?"

He gives me a tight smile and nods. Tears well in my eyes, I look beyond him and the line is still crazy. I bring my gaze back to him.

"Please, please don't go. I would like to talk to you," I plead.

"If you don't mind. I'd like to come by your mama's house tomorrow. I made a promise. I plan to keep it. You take care of these folks waiting to see you. This won't be the last you see of me. I'll be around," he winks and my heart squeezes.

CHAPTER FOUR

Keeping my Word

Parker

I slept for shit in my hotel last night. I couldn't stop thinking about Lakia. It nearly killed me to see the sadness in her eyes when she realized who I was. Her fingers trembled as she signed the copy of her book for her brother.

Once she handed the book over, I wished I had waited at the end of the line. I could see finishing out the signing was going to take a toll on her. Still, I knew if I stuck around in plain sight it would only make it worse.

I watched her from a distance for as long as I could take it. Once my head started to pound, even with my glasses on, I knew it was time for me to leave. Last thing I needed was to forget where my hotel was, while in a city I don't know.

Turning my head to the clock, it lights up 0400hrs. I groan, sitting up with a grunt. I haven't been sleeping much anyhow.

In the hospital, I would lose entire periods of time. Just gone, forgotten. Other times, my vision would go, which led to the new glasses I've been wearing. I lost my shit once, when my vision went to shit and I forgot why I couldn't see or where the fuck I was.

I wouldn't say it out loud to the docs, but I feel like a broken man. I'm here to keep a promise, but I'm not entirely sure I can do what Redding asked of me. Although, I'll die trying—I know that with everything I am.

Blowing out a breath, I rub my eyes. I want to get to Redding's mama's house before breakfast. I need to make a stop or two on the way.

Dragging my ass out of bed, I take a shower. I don't bother to look down at the scarred flesh on my left side. I pushed my body to its limits to get back on my feet. The soldier in me needed to get to my assignment.

My mind turns to the mission ahead of me. I can't get her eyes and lips out of my head. I lean forward, placing my forehead against the shower wall. I can feel my groin tighten, but I don't have time to give it attention.

I also haven't decided how I feel about all of this. I don't know what Redding would think about me desiring his little sister like this. He'd probably kick my damn ass.

I shake the thoughts from my mind and finish up. I need to hit the twenty-four hour gym I found. I noticed I started to limp last night. At times the damage to the nerves sets in and I lose feeling. Docs said if I continue to work at it, the muscle memory may kick in. The damage could have been a lot worse.

I roll my shoulders, focused on the tasks ahead of me. I have a plan and I'll stick to that. First, I need to make myself known to Myles' family. They'll be seeing a lot of me from now on. I want to make them comfortable with my presence.

I'm dressed and out the door fifteen minutes later. I press my lips at the black frames in my hand. I hate these glasses. Memories of high school flood my brain. I wore glasses from grade school all the way to the twelfth grade. My father didn't see the point in me getting contacts. When I turned eighteen, I used the money my mama left me to get laser surgery. What a waste that turned out to be.

I stop myself from crushing the glasses in my palm out of anger. I remind myself—I'm alive and I have my vision. Placing the specs on my face and tossing my gym bag in the passenger seat, I climb into the vehicle I rented. I'll find a place and get a car once I get settled with the family.

My phone rings, bringing me out of my mental planning and musing. I grit my teeth when I see my cousin's name pop up on the screen. Ryder is a good guy, a retired Master Chief Petty Officer. He actually has been here in Texas with his mama and pop for a bit. If he gets wind that I'm in town, I'll never get him out of my hair.

I'm not ready to deal with how I feel about all that's happened. I shift in my seat, not comfortable with ignoring my family, but knowing I'm not ready to answer his call. I sigh when the ringing stops and the phone dings for voicemail.

Begrudgingly, I swipe to listen to the message. I grimace with guilt as my cousin's familiar voice greets my ears. Thoughts of home and my daddy surface. He'd be pissed that I'm avoiding family.

"Jake, you can't dodge me forever. Remember who I am. I know you've been discharged, you were cleared two days ago. I want to hear from your ass," Ryder commands. I can hear him mumble under his breath, as he goes to disconnect the phone line. "Stubborn ass."

A small smile tugs up the side of my lips. I'll call him back later, before he has the entire Navy looking for me. I wouldn't put it past him.

Suddenly, I'm not sure where I'm headed to. I try to remember, but my head fights against me the more I push. I refuse to panic. I know I have important things to do. I look around at the street outside.

Nothing provides me with a clue. Stopping at a light, I sigh, pinching the bridge of my nose. Something catches my eye in the passenger seat. It's my gym bag.

The gym.

I nod to myself. I'm going to the twenty-four-hour gym to blow off some steam and work on my leg. My brows knit.

Come on, Parker. Strategize. Don't let this beat you.

A horn blows behind me, bringing my attention to the green light. I pull off and turn into the first lot I find. I park and pick up my phone. Opening a free note, I make a list of my tasks for the day. When done, I program the GPS on the car for all of my stops and their locations.

You got this.

~B~

Lakia

"Girl, why on earth are you up pacing?" Mama breaks through my thoughts as I peek out the curtains. "Shouldn't you be writing?"

It's seven in the morning. I usually get up to get some writing done at this hour. I should be working on my next book, but

I've been distracted. Parker—as my brother always referred to him—didn't give me a time for when he would arrive. Yet, I've been on pins and needles, waiting for him to appear.

I've been staying at my mother's house for a little over a month now. Those first few weeks were so hard on her. I could see she wasn't taking care of herself. I wanted to be close to her, after Myles'…I still can't even think the words.

The fact that we didn't even have a body to bury makes this all so much harder. I wish there was more I could do to help my mother heal. I still don't know where to begin for myself.

"You're up early," I reply, avoiding her observation.

"I couldn't sleep," she sighs, running a hand through her salt and pepper pixie cut. "It's still not real for me. I can't accept that I've lost my son."

"I know, Mama. I…" my words cutoff in my throat.

"I need to busy myself. I thought I'd make breakfast, while you write," she says, moving to the refrigerator.

I smile. The kitchen is Mama's favorite place to be. She hasn't been in the mood to cook much lately, this is good. I start for my seat at the nook, but the doorbell stops me in my tracks.

"Who could that be," Mama says, starting for the door.

"I'll get it," I wave her off, not telling her it could be a friend of Myles.

My heart pounds as I go. I don't know why I'm reacting like this. I want to talk to Parker. I want to know what happened to my brother, but my racing heart says that I want a whole lot more.

Girl, if you don't get yourself together. Being a sucker for grey eyes and sexy swagger got you in the mess you're in now.

I frown, as I think of Toni's ass. He called me, demanding to know when I'd be returning to my own home. I nearly told him to kiss my ass.

"I hope I didn't offend you yesterday," that sexy rumble from yesterday pulls me from my thoughts.

I blink, tipping my head back to look up at him. He takes my breath away. His black square framed glasses aren't on his face, but hanging from his button down's pocket. Those blue eyes are on clear display, showing off those long black lashes. The way they curl and seem to wisp out have me so damn jealous. Surprisingly, today he has the start of a beard covering his square jaw. Yesterday at the signing, he just had light stubble growing in.

I bite my lip as dirty thoughts of that facial hair between my thighs assault my senses. I can't even remember what he just said to me. His brows knit and he lifts the bags in his hands.

"I stopped for a few things at the grocery store. I wanted to make you guys breakfast, but if you want me to come back later…" he trails off.

"No, no," I shake my head clear. "Please come in. You don't have to make us breakfast."

"I figured it would be a way for you all to get to know me," he says with a sexy crooked smile, before crossing the threshold.

"How did you know I would be here this early," slips out of my mouth, before I can think better of it.

He turns his head, those sharp eyes locking on me. "Your brother asked me to check in on you all if anything ever happened to him. I've been doing all I can from a distance. Now I'm here, I'm thorough in all I do, Ma'am," he replies, his eyes traveling over me.

I don't know why every word that just came out of his mouth sounds so dirty. Maybe it's because he is dripping with sex. It is just oozing off of him.

"Oh," is all I can come up with.

I fight not to slap my hand to my forehead. I pull it together and rush around him to lead him into the kitchen. I can hear Mama moving around in there. I don't know how she's going to feel about this man in her kitchen. I seriously doubt she's going to allow it. I stopped trying years ago.

"Mama, we have company," I say, when she comes into view.

She looks up from the coffeemaker and a gasp leaves her lips. I haven't seen my mama move this fast in eons. Parker sets down the bags in his hands just in time to wrap his arms around her. I watch as his face fills with sorrow and regret. He holds her closely, as she clings to him.

"My son loved you like family. He promised to bring you home the last time I talked to him," she nearly sobs.

"He was my family, Ma'am. Y'all all are," he replies, emotions clear in his voice.

Wrapping my arms around myself, I try to hold it together. His eyes lift from my mama in his arms. She looks so much smaller than him. Tears start to slip free, when he opens an arm to wave me into the hug. My feet are moving without my consent.

I join the hug, wrapping an arm around Mama and one around Parker. I'm blown away at the instant safety I feel. His warmth engulfs me, pulling me into his aura. There is something dark but comforting at the same time. I want to bury myself deeper into it, but I stay stock-still.

"I'd like to make you all breakfast. That way we can get to know each other a bit better," he says after a few moments.

I step out of his hold, bracing myself. I hope Mama will let him down gently. He has been very sweet, but Mama being Mama can be darn right abrasive sometimes.

"Aren't you sweet," my mama turns her face up to smile at him. "Let me know what you need and I'll get out of your way."

My mouth drops open. Then my brows knit. Mama must be taking this harder than I thought. Myles couldn't make his own doggone toast in her kitchen. Heck, it's a fight for me to make Isaac a cup of hot chocolate. I've been ordering out since we've been here or cooking on the few occasions she'll go out to Bingo or Spades with friends.

It's not that she doesn't trust my cooking. She just takes over when you're in her kitchen. I move to take a seat by my laptop at the nook. I have to see this. There is no way she is going to let him cook a full meal in her kitchen.

I watch in stunned silence as she sets him up. My head tilts, as I begin to watch Parker more closely. Texas gets pretty hot for the long sleeve shirt he has on. I'm not surprised when he begins to roll up his right sleeve. What peaks my interest is his hesitation when he goes for his left. In the end, he unbuttons the cuff and rolls it once.

Girl, maybe he has some sexy ass tat that says something naughty he doesn't want Mama to see.

My imagination runs wild. So much so, I don't realize that Mama has joined me at the table. I'm too busy imagining what Parker looks like with his clothes off.

"Girl, you need to close your mouth," my mama snickers.

My head snaps in her direction. I wipe under my mouth to ensure I'm not drooling, causing my mother to throw her head back in a full laugh. It's such a beautiful sound. I don't think I've heard it since the morning we talked on the phone before—

I shut the memory down quickly, wanting to stay in this moment.

I fan my face and lean into Mama. "Lawrt, the man is fine," I whisper.

"That he is. I'm sure he and your brother had the women swooning left and right," she says, with sad eyes that sparkle just a little.

"I can't believe you're letting him in your kitchen," I display my shock.

"A man that fine offers to cook for you, you step out of the way," she shrugs. "Lord, have mercy. I think he is finer with the glasses on."

I turn to see what has my mother nearly drooling this time. Sure enough, Parker has those glasses on. He looks damn sexy and confident in my mother's home. The place is already starting to fill with delicious scents. He looks up from his task and locks eyes with me.

"I was told French toast is your favorite and Isaac loves strawberry pancakes," he says with a slight smile on his lips. His eyes turn to Mama. "Apple and cinnamon oatmeal for you, Ma'am."

It's not questions. He's showing us he knows facts about us. My nipples tighten against my bra. It's the sexiest thing I've ever seen. His confidence in his knowledge and the ease in his movements. It's all mouthwatering.

"You think you can make my oatmeal better than me," I turn to see Mama giving him side eye with her question.

I cover my mouth to hide my smile. This is what I was expecting all along. I think Parker just got himself thrown out of my mama's kitchen.

"No, Ma'am. I don't, but I'm going to try my hardest to get it as close as possible," he gives a small chuckle.

"Oh, no, baby. Let me get in this kitchen," Mama starts to lift from her seat.

"I don't think so, Ma'am," Parker says firmly.

Once again, my mouth pops open. I think he has just gotten his behind thrown out of the house. My eyes volley between the two. Mama is frozen, mid-way out of her seat. Her brow is lifted. Parker lifts a hand to still her wrath.

"I'm going to ask you to trust me. I'll surprise you. I promise," he says, turning on that megawatt smile.

Mama falls for it, easing her way back down into her seat. I'm speechless. Mama doesn't back down or listen to anyone. My son's father is a police officer and she has threatened his life on more than one occasion.

Mama's reaction to Parker is forgotten when I hear a tiny gasp and the halting sound of footy pajamas sliding on the hardwood floor. I see a caramel faced, wide-eyed Isaac staring up at Parker in awe. He breaks into a smile showing his little teeth.

"Uncle Parker," he squeals, causing my heart to squeeze.

"There's my little buddy. I've missed our talks," Parker croons, crouching down to Isaac's height.

My son runs right into his arms. My heart melts in my chest. Myles used to tell me to leave the room and let Isaac have some space while the "men" talked. Isaac loved the time he had with his uncle. I just never knew Parker was such a big part of that time.

Isaac is a lively and bright four-year-old. He doesn't miss a thing. It's one of the reasons I hate the way his father treats him so much. I could give two rats behinds what Toni does to me, but when he makes Isaac promises he knows he's not going to keep, it drives me insane.

"I missed you, too. I miss Uncle Myles. Mommy said he's in heaven and my tablet doesn't reach that far," my son's little sad voice tears my heart to pieces.

Parker gives him a squeeze. His arms tighten so much, I think he might break my son. Isaac's little arms wrap around his neck and he holds him just as tightly.

"I'll be here for you, little buddy. Whatever you need, you come to me just like you would your Uncle Myles," Parker says like a promise.

I frown. I don't want this man making promises to my son he won't keep. His father already does enough of that. Isaac is already crushed that Myles isn't coming back. He was so looking forward to it.

I stand, catching Parker's eyes over Isaac's head. I press my lips and shake my head sternly at him. I'm taken back when Parker's blue eyes darken. He lifts to his feet, taking Isaac with him, hoisting him onto his hip.

"Since, we're all getting to know each other. You should know I always keep my word, Lakia. It's why I'm here. I always say what I mean and mean what I say," he says while looking me straight in the eyes.

Well, damn!

~B~

Parker

I watch Lakia keep her focus on the plate of French toast and turkey bacon in front of her. She's just as gorgeous as she was yesterday, just without any makeup. It's refreshing to see. A fresh face on a beautiful woman.

It's a look I wouldn't mind waking up to. I also wouldn't mind those eyes staring up at me, while I rock into that curvy body. I couldn't take my eyes off of her round ass and hips as she led me into the kitchen earlier.

"I'll be. This oatmeal might just be as good as mine," Ms. Redding hums.

I turn my eyes to her and give a small smile. Her cola colored eyes remind me so much of her son's. They're the exact same. I feel a stab in my chest looking into them.

"I'll tell you my secret someday," I wink.

"Your pancakes are better than mommy's," Isaac sings, while dancing in his seat.

I choke back my laugh, looking over at Lakia who gives me a death glare. I try to straighten my face, but my lips still twitch. She's adorable angry.

"So, where are you staying, Parker?" I turn to answer Ms. Redding's question, finding her watching me intently.

"I have a room at a hotel for now. I'll be looking for something more permanent this week," I reply.

"We have some place for you. Lakia has been thinking about renting the apartment over her garage. She can get you all set up there, since she's going back home this weekend."

"Wait, what? I never said I was going back home," Lakia's face crumbles.

I notice she's not protesting my moving in. I watch her closely, taking in the pout on her full lips. She's definitely more disappointed in her mother putting her out, than in my moving into her property.

"I know you didn't. And while I love you and my little munchkin. I want my house back to myself," Ms. Redding says pointedly.

"Well, dang, Mama," Lakia pouts some more. "You could have told me you were tired of us sooner."

"Girl, you get up all times of the night to hack away on that computer. And good Lord, when you get on the phone with that Kaye and Dean," she shakes her head. "You girls can get on my last nerve."

Lakia bursts into laughter. It's like watching an angel come to life. Her entire face lights up.

"Mama, that's just not right," she says through her laughter.

"It's true. Your husband is going to have to have the patience of a saint," Ms. Redding rolls her eyes.

"Ha! Good thing I'm not planning on marrying," Lakia frowns.

It's the same frown she opened the door with earlier. I'd thought she was disappointed to find me on the other side of the threshold. I can't help but wonder where her brain goes each time she makes that face.

"Girl, T-O-N-I, will not be the end all and be all of your life. The right man will have you more than willing to marry," Ms. Redding waves Lakia off.

That sour frown reappears at the spelling of Isaac's father's name. Now that I think of it, Myles used to make the same sour face when talking about his nephew's father. I think I may now know where Lakia's thoughts keep turning.

I'm a little surprised at how possessive and jealous that makes me. I clench my jaw and flex my left hand under the table. The thought of any other man trying to marry her sends white-hot rage through my veins.

"How soon can I move in?"

The words are out before I process them. Lakia looks over to me as if she's just remembering I'm in the room. She bites her lip and dips her head a little. I feel my cock twitch at the sight.

"It's available whenever you're ready. I usually ask for references and a background check, but you're family," she says softly.

"You are welcome to do the check and I can have references to you within the hour," I respond.

"You will do no such thing," Ms. Redding chides.

"It's not a problem, Ma'am."

"First of all, call me, Coretta," she presses her lips at me. "It's a two bedroom apartment, Myles finished it for her in between deployments. I think he would like knowing you're staying there. Lakia was going to list for seventeen-fifty. Can you handle that?"

"I'll pay for the first six months, if that's okay with you," I say to Lakia, not taking a second to think about it.

"Wow, um, are you sure? That's a lot of money. What if you don't like it?" Lakia's brows pucker in the center of her pretty face.

"I'm sure I'll be fine. I only said six months in advance and not a year, in case you don't like having me so near," I shrug.

"You might as well pay the year, baby," Ms. Redding mutters under her breath.

"Mama," Lakia hisses, her cheeks glowing with warmth.

"Uncle Parker, if you move into our house will you play basketball with me? Oh, and can you read to me at night?" Isaac's eyes sparkle with joy.

"Isaac, I think Mr. Parker has a life of his own," Lakia says gently. "We won't be bothering him."

"You two bother me as much as you want," I say, looking Lakia right in the eyes.

"Yay! Strawberry pancakes on Saturdays, please," Isaac cheers.

A laugh rumbles in my chest, lightening the heavy feeling I've had since waking in Germany. I don't miss the smile Ms. Redding tries to smother, nor do I miss the deer in headlights look on Lakia's face. I have a feeling this is all just hitting her with a dose of reality. I mean to stay, just like I said I am.

CHAPTER FIVE

Limitations

Parker

I stare at the woman across the desk from me trying to remember the answer to the question she just asked me. I roll my lips in frustration. I prayed this wouldn't happen in the middle of this job interview. I have enough money not to work, but I've worked and worked hard all my life.

I was helping my daddy milk the cows by the time I was four. I grit my teeth, pissed that I can pull up that memory, but I can't find the answer to the question at hand. Teaching college courses on strategy and psychology is right up my alley. I want this damn job.

"Take your time. I cleared time for this interview. I understood we might need more time," Dean, Dr. Winsor says gently.

My eyes narrow at her. This entire interview was a huge favor. I finally called my cousin back, and just as I thought he made sure to get involved, while dragging every military and Naval friend and family member into it as well.

"Jake, Commander Parker doesn't lift his head just for anyone. He was very candid with me. I know about your trauma and discharge. The Commander and I go way back," her smile brightens her face, telling a story of its own. "He speaks very highly of you. I think this would be a great position for you. We just need to place a few aides in place."

My jaw works. Commander Parker, or should I say, Uncle Wayne, warned me he would give Dr. Winsor full disclosure on my condition. He and Ryder have done a lot in a short amount of time. I appreciate that.

"Aides?"

"Yes, I believe I can be of assistance to you. I've worked with a few soldiers that have dealt with similar challenges. I may be able to offer you a fresh set of coping skills. First, we'll get you a TA. I also have a few tricks you'll find useful," a warm smile stretches across her brown face. "I think you'll be perfect for this teaching position."

"Okay, I'm listening," I nod my head. "And to answer your question. I taught a few classes in my earlier years in Afghanistan. I considered being a professor a number of times once easing back into civilian life. My mama was a school teacher, before she passed."

I sigh in relief at being able to finally answer the question. Hope blooms. I'm broken, but there are ways to mend me up.

~*B*~

Lakia

It's been a week and a half since Parker moved into the garage apartment and I returned to my home. Funny, Mama came to take Isaac back to her house a day after we returned. If I didn't know my mama so well, I might be offended.

I huff at my computer screen for the millionth time, while I sit in the window seat doing my best to work. Only thing I've managed to do is stare out the window, waiting for Parker to return home. We had coffee together this morning. He seemed so nervous about his interview.

He looked amazing in his black suit and white shirt. I couldn't for the life of me figure out why he'd been so nervous. I was sure he would nail the interview without question. Although, I got the feeling there was something I was missing.

I've come to enjoy the time I get to spend with Parker. He's so polite and attentive. Isaac can't stop talking about him. Mama doesn't live that far away, and Parker has gone by to check on her and my son almost every single day.

At night, when I call to wish my son goodnight, our calls have turned into recaps of his time with Parker. It reminds me so much of the way he would go on and on about his calls with his Uncle Myles. I'm happy for Isaac, but I do hope Parker keeps his word.

I guess that's why I'm as nervous as he was about this job. I know he has given me six months rent up front, but the commitment to a job would be one more thing to keep him rooted here. I keep telling myself my concern is all for Isaac, but in all honesty, I've become invested in having Parker around as much as my son has.

The sound of Parker's F150 pulling into the driveway has me pulling back the curtains again. I peek out to see him stepping from his brand new black truck. It suits him. I thought it the first day he came home with it. Damn if he doesn't look good coming out of it—whether in a suit or in blue jeans and a white thermal shirt.

My mouth goes dry as he starts for my front door. My heart pounds in my chest. When he stops mid-stride, his brows knitting, I stop breathing. Disappointment slams into me when he turns, heading back into his truck.

I can hear my heart hammering; my hands feel all clammy. I watch with baited breath as he fiddles around in his truck. He runs a hand through his hair, seeming to be frustrated. When I see his head lower to the steering wheel, I feel like I'm intruding. Feeling guilty for watching whatever is happening before me, I close the curtain and move to my office to get some work done.

"I hope he got the job," I mutter, as I plop down in my chair, disappointed.

CHAPTER SIX

Sparks

Lakia

I was so excited when Parker told me he got the job. It was the day after the interview. Parker never did come by after whatever happened with him. However, seeing the joy that lit up his eyes the next day made me forget all about the incident.

Parker has a tendency to space out and become broody. Seeing another side of him, a side that I don't think he shares with many, had me wanting to do something special for him. I know he doesn't know many people here—or at least I thought he didn't.

I found out he has family here in Texas, after I decided to throw a barbecue in my backyard. I made up a story about wanting to kick back and celebrate the success of my last book. Parker seemed to buy that and even said he'd invite a few friends and family when I extended the invitation.

What I wasn't expecting was my ex to show up, his damn soapbox in hand. I swear the man thinks he's God's gift to earth. The arrogance that comes off of Toni is unbelievable. When I was young, I thought it was swag. Now, I recognize it as his overinflated ego.

Toni's family hails from Italy. His father was a very proud man. Yet, Toni Sr. was never a prick like his son. I was so sorry when he passed. I think he kept Toni as grounded as anyone could. After his father's death, Toni only got worse.

"You know if you keep looking at him like that, he may arrest you," Mama says from beside me.

"I can't stand him," I hiss. "Look at him, here acting like he's such an active family man. Taking credit for shit he ain't never done."

"Watch your mouth," Mama kisses her teeth. "You lay with a snake expect to get bitten. I warned you about that one from the time you brought him through my door. You had to be hard headed and learn for yourself."

I hold my tongue not wanting to get slapped out here in this heat, in front of all these people. It's not like she's lying. Mama warned me repeatedly about Toni. Not once did I listen to her. I did this to myself.

Mama sighs, bumping me with her hip. "It's not the fall or the amount of times you fall. It's the amount of times you get up and the choices you make once you're standing on solid footing.

"You need to learn to trust yourself again. The Universe will handle that fool, if I don't do it first," she finishes with narrowed eyes shooting daggers in Toni's direction.

"What am I going to do with you," I chuckle.

"Baby, the question is what are you going to do about that man that can't keep his eyes off of you when he's around?"

"What man?" I ask innocently.

"So, I'm a fool now?"

"No," I mutter.

"Where is he, by the way? You didn't run him off, did you? I didn't see his truck when I arrived," Mama looks around the backyard.

"I forgot a few things. He made a store run," I shrug.

"Well, I'll be damned. It looks like he did more than go on a store run. If I were a few years younger," Mama fans herself.

I look up to see what she's talking about. My mouth drops open, as I follow her line of sight. Parker and a group of men I don't know are all walking into my backyard, looking like a wet dream. There isn't one ugly mug in the crew. They all look like they could be military or something.

You can't tell me I'm not watching a movie. The part when all the hot heroes arrive to kick ass. Parker is at the center of the gang, looking sexy as hell.

Even in the sleeved t-shirt he has on, I can make out his muscled chest and arms. His denim jeans are hugging those thighs just right as always. He has on shades instead of his glasses and it's a nice look.

All of the men head straight over to me and Mama. My eyes bounce over them all before landing on Parker again. He has a sexy grin on his full lips and a twinkle in his eyes, as he looks over his glasses.

"I invited my cousin, but he got it in his mind to bring the entire clan," Parker grumbles and shoots a mock glare at the one I assume to be his cousin.

I can see the resemblance. Though, his eyes are more violet than blue and his blonde hair is just a bit longer than a buzz cut, he looks like Parker in the face. Their noses and lips are very similar.

"Ryder, this is Lakia," Parker introduces.

"It's a pleasure to meet you, Darlin'."

"It's nice to meet you. I'm so glad you could all make it," I beam.

Parker goes to say something else, but the atmosphere shifts and I can feel a burning glare at my back. I close my eyes, the feeling of all hell breaking loose taking over me.

~B~

Parker

I know it's him the moment I set eyes on him. His arrogance oozes off of him. I don't miss the fact that as he saunters our way, he plucks Isaac up and carries him along with him. It's a statement. He thinks he's marking his territory.

I find that amusing. Not once, since I've been living here, have I seen him around. The fool is a clown just like Myles described him.

"Uncle Parker," Isaac squeals with joy, wiggling free from his father's arms.

I grin. Perfect example of when a power play goes wrong. I bend and pick the young boy up. I can't tell you how much it warms my heart when he wraps his arms around my neck. This little kid has grown on me fast.

"What's up, Buddy?" I croon, not taking my eyes off the asshole glaring back at me.

"Did you get the cake and ice cream? Mommy promised you were picking it up," Isaac says hopefully.

"I got it right here, little dude," Jax croons, holding up the cake and bags he's carrying.

Jax entered the air force when Ryder joined the Navy. We all grew up together. All of these guys are like brothers to me. Every one of these men with me have served our country in one way or another. The six of us have been through enough to fill a book.

"Hi, I'm Isaac."

I chuckle at the way Isaac puffs out his chest. His eyes sparkle, as he looks around at the five men surrounding me. Max reaches out to shake Isaac's hand.

"Hey, Isaac, nice to meet you. Put it there, I'm Max," the big guy says, with a broad grin on his almond colored face.

"Up top big guy," Alvarez croons, lifting his hand.

Isaac beams giving him a high five. I grin when Doc steps forward, ruffling Isaac's short curls. Doc is a big softy when it comes to kids.

"I'm Doc, Kid. Nice to meet you," he says, his green eyes twinkling with mirth as he lowers his voice. "We'll get into some trouble later."

"Stay away from him," I whisper in Isaac's ear, tickling his side.

"You sure do look cozy with *my* family," a gruff voice interrupts Isaac's laughter.

I lift my eyes from Isaac, raising a brow. This asshole is bolder than I thought. He has an arm around Lakia's shoulders, while she stands as stiff as a board.

I squat to put Isaac down, lifting to my full height again. I look at the arm the piece of shit has on Lakia, if looks could kill his arm would fall off and be on the ground plagued with rigor mortis.

"I'm sorry, you are?" I reply, knowing very well who he is.

His jaw ticks, a vein pops in his forehead. When Lakia shrugs him off her shoulder and steps away, his face reddens with anger. His fists ball as he glares at her, causing me to step in front of her.

"I'm Isaac's father and Lakia's man," he grits out.

"Toni, you're Isaac's father," Lakia corrects.

He flinches at her words, narrowing his eyes at her. I don't like the look he's giving her. It's clear in their ridged stances that none of the guys do either. Although, they hold back to allow me to handle this.

"Funny, as long as I've been around I haven't seen you once," I shrug.

"But I've seen you. How's that new job and that fine Dr. Winsor you're always around?"

I want to punch the smug grin on his lips clear off his face. I step forward so that when I lower my voice he's the only one that can hear me. His eyes grow harder, his face deepens to another shade of red under his olive tone. It's evident he's not used to being challenged.

"I'm the motherfucker that makes nightmares behave. You sure you want to fuck with me?" I say calm and coolly.

"I don't have nightmares because I don't sleep. I'm always awake and watching. Stay away from what's mine, *soldier*," he hisses back at me.

"Ain't shit around here yours. You must be mighty tired from that lack of sleep. Fuck around and I'll rock that ass to sleep for you, boy. I give two fucks about that badge you like hiding behind," I bare my teeth in a smile, when he realizes I do know who he is. I wink at him. "I've learned to sleep with my eyes open. That way I'm always ready to protect what's mine. Oh, and when I protect…that means annihilate. I don't give second chances."

The bastard flexes, as if he is about to throw a punch, but I'm ready. What I don't expect is Lakia jumping in the middle. She shoves at Toni's chest, wiggling her curvy body between us. I'm pissed, but my body still reacts to her soft ass pressed to my front.

"You will not disrespect my house or my guest. If you don't know how to act you can leave," she hisses low. "Think about the example you're showing to your son. He's watching you."

Toni looks over my shoulder, a sour frown replacing the raging one from seconds ago. He turns his eyes back to Lakia, his jaw working for a moment. His eyes then lift to mine.

"We'll see each other again," he tosses my way, before exiting the backyard, without a backward glance.

"Pussy," I mutter.

Lakia spins to look up at me, her eyes narrowed. I search her face, loving the anger I see there. I want to see that passion, when she's writhing beneath me.

I forget myself and those around us. Placing a hand on her hip, I pull her into my heat. I want to taste those full lips, but I stop a breath away from them when I dip my head.

"Parker?" she gasps, quietly.

"Just tell me one thing, has he ever put a hand on you?"

She turns her head away from me. It's all the answer I need. I kiss the side of her temple, releasing my hold on her hip. I go to step around her, but her small hand on my wrist stops me.

"I've walked away from all of that. It's not worth the trouble he'll cause. Let it go. I wasn't a victim. Myles taught me well.

Toni got what he deserved, and he never tried it again," she whispers.

"That's not good enough for me, Sweetheart. Not by a long shot," I shake my head and start to pull away.

"Well, today it's going to have to be," she says with a sexy smile on her lips, wrapping both her hands around my wrist, tugging me to the center of the yard where a few others are dancing.

I'm hesitant at first. I want to turn and go beat the shit out of that asshole, but when those cola eyes sparkle up at me and those lush lips turn up into a megawatt smile—I can't find it in me to pull myself away. It's not a couple's dance, but Lakia still places herself in front of me so we move as one.

I know enough about line dancing to pick up the version they're doing. Lakia looks up at me, throwing her head back in laughter, as I grip her hips and follow their sway. I stay in time the best I can with her rocking and bumping against me.

I can feel my body reacting to hers again. When she sucks her bottom lip into her mouth, I know she can feel it too. The tension around us feels like a whip cracking through the air. I lift a brow, silently asking if she knows what she's getting herself into.

"You're dangerous, Parker, but I think I'm crazy because I'm going to run into this fire with a smile on my face. I've made that decision already," she whispers up at me.

I lean into her ear. "Fires leave scars, Baby. You ready to see what that looks like?"

"I ain't never scared," she winks.

We'll see about that.

CHAPTER SEVEN

Jealous Ex

Lakia

I haven't been able to stop smiling all weekend. Parker left for a trip with his friends, but not before we danced the day and night away at the barbecue. I haven't had that much fun in years. I mean, it's two days later and I can still feel him pressed against me.

I keep asking myself if it's weird that I miss him. He looked a little reluctant to leave that evening, but I could see that his cousin and friends were determined to take him away. I'll admit, I've been a little jealous, wondering if all those fine ass men took off to find a few women to bring them pleasure.

I don't have any claim on Parker, but I think I made it very clear that I'm more than interested in him. I'm usually not that bold, but the way he was ready to defend me, and the way he stood up to Toni, totally turned me on. Toni is no chump, but it looked like he met his match in Parker.

I shake the memory away, laughing at myself. That entire scene just made it into my latest book. I've been up since five, smiling and laughing all morning as I work. I gave up on sleep as my characters nudged at my brain for me to get some of this stuff on the page.

I look up to see that it's nine in the morning already. My smile broadens when I hear Parker's truck pull in. Or at least, I thought it was Parker's truck, until I get up and peek out the window.

I curse under my breath and press my lips. I should've known his ass would be showing up at some point. It dawned on me after the fact that he's been sniffing around more since Parker moved into the garage apartment.

Toni has another thing coming if he thinks he's going to dictate my life. It's one of the main reasons we didn't work out. I refused to let him manipulate, dictate, control, and take over my life. All it took was that one time he put his hands on me and it all became clear. He was never the man I thought he was.

All of the signs were there, showing up at my job, trying to tell me which friends I could and couldn't hang around with, and in the end trying to drive a wedge between me and my family. He went too far the moment he tried to make my mama and brother into the villains. I felt so stupid for taking so long to see what they were trying to tell me all along.

"Why don't you look happier to see me?" He croons when I open the front door.

"Why should I be?"

I fold my arms over my chest, blocking the entryway. Toni lifts his arms, grasping the doorjamb above our heads. He's not nearly as tall as Parker, but he still towers over me just a bit. I'm not intimidated, although, I know that's his intention.

"You going to just stand there, Darlin' or are you going to let me in?"

"You're still on that side so that should give you my answer," I lift a brow to emphasize my point.

Toni drops the façade and that nasty glare comes out. It's the look I know all too well. I place my hands on my hips, ready to go a round or two with him.

"You know, I let you get away with that mouth for way too long. You don't have your big brother to threaten me with anymore. Not that I gave a fuck before, but if I were you, I'd tread more carefully," he growls in my face.

I feel rage fill me, my arms fall to my sides as my fists ball. I was telling Parker the truth. The one time Toni did put his hands on me, I was not the one that looked like they were in a fight. I laughed my ass off at the bullshit story he told his partner. A story that happened to get back to me through a mutual friend.

"Toni, I'm so over you and your bullshit. You're not God's gift to women, you're a shitty father, you were barely a decent boyfriend in the beginning. Get off my porch and go find someone that wants to entertain your bullshit. I'm not biting, I have shit to do," I go to slam the door in his face, but he throws his body in the way, pushing it open.

"You want me out of the way all of a sudden so you can fuck that soldier, don't you?" He snarls.

I knit my brows, glaring up at him. "I've been single for three and a half years. I don't need you out of the way to fuck anybody," I snap back.

He grasps my face between his large fingers, biting into my flesh. I try to pull back, but his hold only tightens. He lowers his lips to mine and forces a rough kiss, breaking the kiss just as I get ready to bite his ass.

"You're not single. You've never been single. You don't even know who that piece of shit is, but you've allowed him in my son's life. I'm warning you. Get rid of him," he commands, releasing me with so much force I stumble back.

I don't get to respond as I straighten up. He's already strolled off, climbing back into his police SUV. I narrow my eyes at his partner sitting in the passenger seat.

Coward, can't even look me in the eyes.

CHAPTER EIGHT

Come Here

Parker

Two months later...

It's been two months since the day of the barbecue. I thought things would be different when I returned for my little trip with the boys. I was actually looking forward to my return.

However, Lakia has been closed off since I got back. To be honest, she's always pissed off and stressed. I haven't pushed to make her talk to me. Although, we've had our little talks in the past, I don't want to push the limits of our budding relationship.

I figured it's all been work related. She has mentioned deadlines a time or two. Yet, I notice she's been taking almost daily trips out of the house. I haven't asked about them because I don't have those rights, but they have peaked my interest.

I've been tempted to follow her, but this new professor position is more demanding than I thought it would be. Even now I have notes I'm putting together for tomorrow's lecture. With my schedule, I've been telling myself that maybe this is all for the best. Myles isn't here for me to ask for his blessing to date his sister and I don't know how he would have felt about it.

So many scenarios have run through my head. It's the other reason I've backed off and allowed Lakia to pull away from me. I've never been indecisive. This is all new territory for me. I don't like it. I know what I want, it's only a matter of time before I allow myself to have it.

I blow out a breath. I haven't been able to concentrate. I had dinner with Lakia and Isaac tonight and something was off. My instincts tell me to go back over there and check in on her. I stop debating it. Tossing my postcards aside and shutting down my laptop, I head out of my apartment for the main house.

~B~

Lakia

I slam another dish into the dishwasher. I'm frustrated to the max. Toni has been dipping out on Isaac repeatedly in the last few weeks. He calls him to get him all excited about spending time together, only to bow out at the last minute.

That crap has me livid, but what I'm totally pissed about is the fact that he has the nerve to be pissed with me because the last two times he's called, Isaac has declined speaking to him. I told him our son is no one's fool. My little baby has had enough. I won't make him talk to Toni if he doesn't want to.

I never talk poorly of my son's father in front of my child. I've allowed him to make his own decision concerning Toni, but even at four he understands his father is a grade A asshole. Children can be more perceptive than we as adults think.

Toni's trying to punish me through our son. He has no idea, he is just fueling me in the process. I watched YouTube video after YouTube video on how to build and secure my own hidden lock boxes. I've built one at every entrance of my home and I have a licensed piece in each one.

I'm not even worried about Toni finding out about the firearms I've recently purchased. Hopefully, the knowledge will show him how serious I am. I go to target practice nearly every day, just before hitting the gym. I'm not playing with this man. I'm tired of it.

His mention of my brother made me aware that he feels he can take being a bully to the next level. I refuse to live like that. I loathe that Toni thinks I'm some weak southern bell that'll wilt under him.

"Son of a bitch," I slam another fork in the dishwasher.

"I'm sure I didn't do anything to deserve that," my nipples harden at the sound of his voice.

My other issue.

I've been so sexually frustrated. I don't want to drag Parker in the middle of this. I've seen how close to flying off the handle he was when he asked if Toni ever put his hands on me. He doesn't need to place himself in Toni's crosshairs for me.

I grasp the edges of the kitchen sink and drop my head between my shoulders. Parker places his hands on my shoulder blades and starts to massage. I sigh and roll my tense upper body into his strong hold.

He moves closer, pressing his body to mine. I don't move away like I know I should. Something in my mind tells me that once Parker places his claim on me, he'll be a part of every aspect of my life. Not in the creepy way Toni has been asserting himself, but in a caring, protective, and loving way.

I moan when his lips meet my neck. Again, I ignore my brain telling me to run. Instead, I push back and wiggle against the hard bulge growing into me. I can't help biting my lip, while thinking about how large he's felt every time he's swelled against me.

"You left the door unlocked. I thought I told you about that," he whispers in my ear.

"Isaac wanted to be a big boy and throw out the trash, I didn't check the lock behind him," I breathe.

"Is he asleep?"

"Yes."

"Good, go sit on the couch. I'll finish up in here," he commands.

I turn to face him and his hands slide down to my waist. His blue eyes lock on mine, saying a million things without a word having to be spoken. I lift on my toes and kiss his cheek, before following his orders.

I'm bone tired and so over fighting my feelings for him. I flop on the couch and throw my head back over the arm. I dig my hands into my hair and close my eyes. I groan when I think about the deadline that's riding my ass. I've been too stressed to think about where I want this book to go.

My phone rings startling me. I look at the time and sigh. I totally forgot that I'd planned a call with Kaye and Dean. When one of us hits a wall with writer's block, we usually get on the line together to work a little sister magic. It's why I love my girls.

"Hey, ladies," I answer the phone, placing it on speaker phone.

"Girl, you sound exhausted," Dean's voice chimes through the line.

"That assumption would be just about right," I huff.

"I feel you. It's been a long day," Kaye yawns.

"How's baby boy?" I ask with a smile.

"He's doing fine, getting on my last nerve," she chuckles. "How's Isaac? I saw the pics you posted, he's getting so big."

"He's a little monster, rushing to become a man," I laugh.

"Hold up, I have questions about the pics your mother posted. I know what Toni looks like and that man in those pics was not Toni. Who's the cutie in the glasses?" Dean interjects.

"I so didn't want to ask, but I saw those too," Kaye giggles tiredly.

"Uh-uh, not now," I murmur, my eyes looking towards the kitchen.

"Mm, sounds to me like someone has company," Dean sings.

"I hate to waste your guys' time, but I'm too tired to even think tonight," I sidestep Dean's comment.

"That deadline is about to fry your ass, Boo. You sure you don't want to at least hash it out?" Dean asks.

"Not tonight," I yawn.

"Well, I'm here when you need," Kaye yawns back. "I'm going to head to bed, Ladies. Love you both."

"Love you too, Girl," I smile.

"Well, personally. I hate you both. Y'all both fucking and I'm not," Dean grumbles.

"No comment," Kaye giggles, hanging up.

I laugh hard, not even acknowledging Dean's comment. Yeah, I know all about Kaye's dirty little secret. I don't judge her. She writes some fire based off of her muse. I wish I was getting it as good as she is. Her pen sets the pages ablaze just like her pen name suggests. Them sheets are a victim of black smoke whenever she gets a chance.

I sigh as the line goes dead, following Dean's laughter. Both of my friends moving on with their lives for the night. I close my eyes again. Dean's words ringing in my head. That deadline is frying my ass. I have got to get my shit together.

I jump, startled when my ankles are lifted from the couch. My eyes open to deep blues, staring back at me. Parker takes a seat, placing my legs across his lap.

"I'm ready to listen when you're ready to talk," his sexy voice rambles.

"About?" I shrug, trying not to sound exhausted.

"I'll be straight with you. I don't play games. I've been there, done that. I like you. I want you. I get the feeling you feel the same. So, you can tell me what's going on or we can talk about something else, but don't try to play me for a fool," Parker says, while massaging my foot with his strong hand.

I just stare, at a loss for words. I groan when he hits a sweet spot on the sole of my foot. Embarrassed, I try to pull back, but he doesn't let me.

His intense eyes remain on me. His hands work magic, while he seems to be waiting out my response. I take a deep breath.

I've learned Parker is very much like my big brother. When they set their minds to something they're tenacious. The determined look in his eyes tells me his mind is definitely set.

"I'm stressed. I have a lot on my plate and I have deadlines to meet," I reply.

"What has you stressed other than the deadlines," he lifts a brow.

I growl. "My deadbeat baby daddy," I roll my eyes.

"Some folks you'll never be able to change. You're a great mama. Isaac is well loved and taken care of. If Toni can't get his act together that shouldn't take away from your life," he says honestly.

I rub my temples. "All easier said. You know. He picks and chooses when he wants to be involved. Always at my inconvenience," I pause and huff. "Can we talk about something else, anything else."

"Come here," he responds, sending shockwaves through my system.

I hesitate for a single moment, before shifting and crawling closer to him. His large hand tugs me into his lap. I stare into his eyes, cupping my hands around his neck. It dawns on me that he's not wearing his glasses.

I tilt my head to the side, taking a good look into his eyes. Suddenly, I feel like I'm falling into them. Their depths are so deep. I almost feel like he's telling me to dive in.

"Show me," I whisper, pleading for him to reveal himself to me.

"It ain't pretty, gorgeous," he says almost sounding pained.

"It never is. Show me."

The words are just barely out, before his lips capture mine. It's the most passionate and demanding kiss I've ever experienced. My fingers slide up into his hair, curling into the silky strains. It's been way too long since I've been with a man. I can't keep myself from rocking in his lap. His hands go from my hips to my backside. His grip is so tight, I feel like he might tear right through my jeans.

"Damn, you taste better than I thought you would," he groans against my lips.

"Please," I plead, not sure what I'm pleading for—more of his kisses or more of his voice rumbling through my body.

I just know I need more. His hands move under my t-shirt cupping my breasts. When his thumbs flick my pebbled buds, I whimper with need.

"I want to see you," he rasps.

"Mommy," Isaac's cry fills the air.

I whimper and not in pleasure. I place my forehead to Parker's and almost burst into tears. My son has been spending so much time at my mama's, for a split moment, I forgot he was in his room sleeping.

"I'm sorry," I whisper.

"Nothing to be sorry about," he shakes his head. "I'll be right here. We can hash out that story of yours when you get back."

My face breaks into a huge smile and my heart stutters. I'm falling for him. I'm falling for him hard.

CHAPTER NINE

I Got This

Parker

We've been up all night. Once Lakia started to talk about her book, her brain just took off. She's been talking to herself and typing for hours. We've been sitting on the couch, her between my legs, while her fingers fly across the keys.

I've inhaled her hair all night, savoring her scent. I have a class to teach this afternoon, but I can't seem to pull myself off this couch. Not when I'd rather be here, watching her in her element.

"Oh, God, Parker. Look at the time," Lakia turns her face up at me and gasps, pulling me from my own musings.

"Did you reach a stopping point," I ask, kissing her temple.

"No, but Isaac will be up soon. I'll make him breakfast and then I can get back to it," she replies, but I can see the longing in her eyes to continue.

I peck her lips. "Keep working. Isaac and I will take care of ourselves. He can come with me today."

"What? You're teaching today," she wrinkles her brows.

"And he can be my assistant," I shrug.

"You don't have to do that."

"That's a matter of opinion," I smile, pecking her lips before reluctantly peeling myself away from her and the couch.

"I owe you big time. Thank you so much. I think I can wrap this one up now," she says, looking at her computer screen with bright eyes.

All the exhaustion from last night has disappeared. I know I've found what makes Lakia happy. Her books are a place of happiness for her. I lean to kiss the top of her head once more.

"You can make it up to me at dinner," I wink when I straighten up.

"Won't you be drained by dinner?" She asks with concern.

"I could go another seventy-two hours."

I grin when her eyes fill with lust. My own thoughts go to the taste and the feel of her. One taste and I know I want a whole lot more.

"Get back to work, I got this," I order, heading for the kitchen to make breakfast.

I peek in the rearview mirror, at Isaac beaming happily in the back of my truck. I think I've enjoyed our day together more than he has. The students were taken with the little guy from the moment we entered class.

My mind has been circling the thought of this being my life. A son, maybe a few more kids and Lakia as my wife. I once swore I'd never try to go there again. Now, it's been all I can think about all day.

I want a baby with those cola colored eyes and brown skin. I want to come home every night to watch my wife create stories she loves, while she rests against my chest.

"Can we do this again?" Isaac calls from the back seat.

Just as they say great minds think alike. I look in the mirror and smile back at him. The plea in his eyes hits me in my damaged heart.

"We sure can," I reply, looking back, as I stop at a light.

"Yes," he pumps his little fist.

"Want to help me make dinner for your mommy tonight?"

"Yeah!" he gushes. "We have to make her favorite."

"Oh, yeah? And what's that," I chuckle.

"Curry chicken with rice and peas," he says, I look in the mirror to see his serious face, as he nods at his words.

"Well, then curry chicken it is," I laugh.

~B~

Lakia

I wake to the house filled with delicious aromas. I crashed sometime after three o'clock this afternoon. Parker sent me a few texts with pictures of Isaac enjoying himself on the college campus and in the classroom. My heart swelled to see my baby having so much fun with a male role model.

Missing my son and Parker the instant the sleep clears from my brain, I drag my body from the bed and jump into the shower. After lotioning my body, putting on some lip gloss and my favorite perfume, I get dressed. I make my way to where the mouthwatering smells are coming from. When I turn into the kitchen, I find Isaac and Parker setting bowls down on the table.

"Hey, cutie pie," I sing to Isaac, when he runs over to hug my legs.

"Hey, Mommy. You have to see what we made," he sings.

"Is that right," I reply, allowing him to pull me the rest of the way to the table.

Parker places the last bowl down on the table, before turning his attention to me. I lift a brow at him, with a teasing smile on my lips. He returns my look with a questioning one of his own. I smile and shake my head at him.

"You made cornbread?" I try to keep the mirth from my face and tone.

He narrows his eyes at me, but I see the smile playing around his lips. He pulls the chair in front of the last bowl he placed on the table. I bite my lip looking between him and the tasty looking food before me.

"Just sit down," he rumbles next to my ear, using his big body to block Isaac's view to quickly nip at my lobe and swiftly pat my ass.

I laugh, sliding into the seat. When he reaches for my shoulder to give a gentle squeeze, I feel a ping of disappointment. I was expecting him to kiss the top of my head, temple or nose, like he did a million times last night. When I look across the table, I see my son watching us intently, understanding hits. Isaac's eyes are so full of happiness and dare I say hope.

I watch his eyes follow Parker as he takes his seat as if he's watching a real live superhero in his home. I feel a sharp pain in my chest. It dawns on me that the last few times Isaac has seen his father he has become so disengaged.

"So how did work go today?" Parker asks, pulling my attention.

"It was great, I typed the end!" I gush.

My exclamation is met by a chorus of cheers. Parker holds up both his hands for Isaac and I to give him five. Isaac slaps his hand, before doing a little dance in his seat.

"Go, Mommy," he sings. "We have to get you gold stars like I get when I do good at daycare."

I roll my lips and nod my head at him. He is too adorable. He looks to Parker for confirmation and beams when he receives a sage nod of approval.

"We'll have to do something special this week while I wait on edits," I smile at him.

"First, you have to eat what we made you," he replies excitedly.

I look down at the bowl in front of me. It looks great. The sauce is not too runny and not so thick it looks like mashed potatoes. Everyone thinks they can make curry, but not many have a clue.

I peek out of the corner of my eyes to see Parker peering at me through his glasses. Just to be snarky, I reach for the cornbread first. Breaking off a piece, I pop it in my mouth.

The flavors that burst in my mouth take me on a journey through my childhood. Church dinners, barbecues, celebration dinners, they all flood my senses. I moan, sagging into myself. All I need is a warm fuzzy blanket and I'd be thrown back in time, when Mama would make me soup and cornbread to make me feel better.

"I think she likes it," I hear Isaac whisper, causing me to realize I've closed my eyes and gone into my own world.

"Amazing, you must have made it," I tease.

"Nope, it was all Uncle Parker. I helped stir the curry chicken and poured the coconut milk in the rice and peas. You have to taste it too," Isaac says anxiously.

I quickly lift my spoon and dig in. I take my first bite and it's delicious. The right note of everything. My mouth salivates for more even as I chew.

"I think we impressed her, Buddy. You won that ice cream," Parker chuckles.

"I told you we would," my son says with his chest puffed up.

"I couldn't have done it without you," Parker reaches to ruffle Isaac's curls.

"Ice cream will be my treat," I chime in.

They both cheer, bringing me to a fit of laughter. It's then that I notice the stress is gone. I haven't felt it since last night. I think Parker might be good for us. Yet another reason I'll have to handle Toni sooner rather than later.

CHAPTER TEN

Here for You

Lakia

I've been on cloud nine for the last two weeks, but today is hitting me so hard. While others are out having fun at barbecues, this day brings me so much pain. I was flooded with memories of my brother from the time I woke up.

I didn't think a simple holiday would dredge up so much hurt. I can still recall the laughter in my brother's voice the last time we talked. He'd been teasing me about my lack of adult life.

Myles knew I loved to spend time with my books. I can get lost in them for days. When it's not my books, it's my son. I rarely go out. I never bothered to date, I just don't have time for it.

I remember Myles' promise that day. He laughed his butt off when I told him I spent my twenty-eighth birthday at Chuck E.

Cheese's with my son. It took almost two full minutes for him to calm down.

"Sis, when your big bro gets home, he's going to teach you how to have a life. I'm going to drag Parker's ass to Texas and we're going to show you how to live. You had a kid, Kia. You didn't die," he chuckled.

Another tear slips free as I play the conversation in my head again and again. I know today must be hard on Mama. She came for Isaac last night, but it dawned on me this morning that she did it as a distraction. I should have known when she kept going on and on about the plans she had for them.

I'm glad my son can give her the reprieve she needs. I've found my way into a bottle of wine. Okay, I may have found myself in the bottom of a few bottles. They have been my solace in the midst of my hurt.

I've picked up my phone to text Parker a hundred times, but I've cut myself off from sending a drunken text each time. I'm still focused enough not to want to embarrass myself. Although, it stings that I haven't heard from him today.

I look out of the window from my perch on the bench seat. The lights are all off in my house, I haven't moved since the sun went down. However, I can see the lights are on in Parker's place.

"What are you doing in there?" I wonder aloud.

I blow out a breath, no longer wanting to be alone—and I mean that in so many ways. Decision made, I get up to stumble to my room to freshen up. I change out of my jean shorts and tank top, into a strapless sundress. I look in the mirror and start to feel a little self-conscious.

Before Isaac, I was a slim thick chick. Over the years, I've become more curvy thick, with some extra cushion. I don't mind. Although Toni has made comments before about me letting myself go. I frown at that thought and stick my tongue out at my reflection.

I love every inch of me and the next man to have the privilege of all of this, will do the same or he can kick rocks right along with Toni. I giggle at my thoughts sounding more like Dean than me. Her sassy New Yorker vibe tends to wear off on others.

I brush my hair back into a ponytail, letting my twist out, and create a bushy bun on top of my head. Parker has seen it all. I don't have anything to hide from him. I grin when that thought enters my mind.

Forgetting everything else, I move quickly to get up to Parker's apartment. I don't stop to think about what I'm doing. I'm knocking at the front door before I know it.

When he doesn't answer right away, I knit my brows and turn to see his truck is in the driveway. My heart sinks, I never thought about him already having company. I mean, we've never discussed being exclusive or anything like that. I guess I've just been assuming, with the amount of time he spends with me and my son.

I drop my head and turn to leave. Before I can get in two steps to lead me away, a large arm snakes around my waist, pulling me back into a warm firm body. I exhale and sag into the warmth of him.

"Darlin', I'm more fucked up than usual today," his voice gruffly greets my ear. "I started not to open up, but I think I need you."

I can smell the alcohol on his breath. I guess I'm not the only one that found comfort in a bottle today. I turn in his arms; his eyes are red and his glasses are nowhere in sight.

He's still the most gorgeous man I've ever seen. I push my fingers through the front of his hair. He captures my palm, pressing his lips to it. My eyes flutter closed while my entire body starts to hum. The butterflies in my belly lift off into a wild frenzy.

I feel more than see when he wraps his arms around my waist, tugging me into the apartment with him. The door closes behind me, just before my back meets hard with the mahogany. My eyes flutter open to find him staring down at me.

"I hope your brother can forgive me for this," he murmurs, just before his lips lock to mine in a searing kiss.

I feel my heart open up to him and pour out all my secrets in just a single kiss. My toes curl in my sandals. My panties are soaked to the point of ruin. I'm crazed for this man, I crave him with everything I am.

I know it's clear we are both aching inside, but I won't be stopping to point that out. We need each other. I want to get lost in him for a few hours, or days if I could. I want to be the one to help him with the demons I know are riding his back.

I know he wants the same as I feel his hands everywhere, as if he hasn't decided where he wants to touch more. My breasts ache for his touch. I almost cry out with joy when he tugs down the top of my dress and strapless bra in one swift motion.

My breasts bounce free, Parker has broken the kiss to watch the action. His big hands rise to cup my mounds, pinching my hardened nipples between his thumbs and forefingers. I shiver and whimper at the sweet torture.

My heart races and my throat becomes dry when I see the lust and hunger in his eyes. I reach to push the dress the rest of the way down, but he grasps my hands and shakes his head.

Releasing one hand, he lifts my chin with his fingertips. "I've wanted to undress you for so long. Let me savor this."

I nod, reaching for his belt instead. His lips return to the sweet torture he's creating, as he sips from my lips. I manage to tug his belt free and unzip his pants, while releasing moans of anticipation and pleasure.

Parker's lips move to my neck as his hands slowly skim over my skin, pushing my dress from my body. He leisurely squats down in front of me, hooking his fingers into my panties, peeling them from my body.

I shyly rub my thighs together, as I shift beneath his hot gaze. I can feel my slickness coat my legs. Parker uses his hand to pry my limbs open at the juncture encasing my secret place. I convulse when his hot hand brushes my folds.

I open for him, spreading my legs. Parker surprises me. In a quick move, he spins, placing his back to the door, sitting on his backside, and grasping the front of my thighs. Gently, he moves me forward. A hand slides around to the back of my thigh, gliding up over my butt cheek, then carefully bending me over at the waist. My ass is now fully in his face.

"Parker," I cry out, when his tongue takes a slow trip through my juices.

I clasp the backs of my calves, peeking up at him through my own legs. His hooded eyes peer down at me. It's the sexiest thing I've ever seen. He opens his mouth wider and begins to really feast on me.

I relax my body and start to slow wine on his face. I dance to the rhythm he has set with his fingers, tongue, and lips. He plucks my body to the perfect crescendo, sending me gushing all over his face.

My legs weaken, my hands grasp his thighs beneath me. His arm bands around me, bringing me down into his lap. I feel him press against my folds and start to rock on instinct. I can feel his heat searing through his boxers.

I catch my breath, while he kisses my neck and kneads my breasts. His hand clasps beneath my chin turning my face to his. He thoroughly devours my face just like he did my pussy. I nearly come again from the kiss alone.

I can taste myself on his lips and tongue. He makes sure of it, leaving no corner of my mouth untouched. He searches my cavern with precision.

I want nothing more than to remove the fabric separating us and ride him until I can't anymore, but my inner freak has other plans. She feels challenged by Parker, and who am I to tell her not to claim what's hers.

I break away from the kiss, reaching to free him from his boxers. He lifts his hips to help me push them down and away. That's when I feel his body stiffen. It's as if he's just realizing what he's done.

I understand right away. His left leg has scar tissue running up the side and along some of the front. The man I've seen as perfect from the first time I laid eyes on him in the flesh, is actually flawed.

My mind goes into overdrive. As hot as it gets in Texas, Parker always has on a long sleeve shirt. If he rolls up his sleeves, it's never on the left side, only on the right. I've never seen him in shorts.

My heart aches. I get the feeling this all came from that last mission he was on with my brother. I dip my head to kiss the scarred flesh. I know in my heart that he earned them, while trying to keep my big brother safe.

Tears try to spill over, but I fight them back. I continue to kiss a trail back up to his thigh. He starts to relax with each kiss.

I think I surprise Parker this time. I lift my body, while staying bent in half. Almost the same position I was in when he devoured my core. I use my legs and arms to support me as I walk up the wall behind him, positioning my face over his shaft.

"Fuck, Baby," Parker hisses into my folds.

I lower my mouth onto him the same time his arms collapse around my waist and his face buries into my weeping center. I take on the challenge of Parker's thick hardness. He has a nice length and girth. I want to giggle out loud when I think of how pissed Toni would be to know he's totally been out done—and that's saying a lot.

Instead of allowing those foolish thoughts to distract me, I bob like my life is counting on it. I soak his dick with each pass, slurping and licking. I get bold and deep throat him a couple of times. Gagging, but too crazed with lust to care. He tastes so good, I want to suck the flavor off of him. I know, it shows when he throws his head back and groans, his arms tightening around me.

"Shit, Lakia, I've never...ah, fuck," he growls.

I bet he's never and never will again from anyone but me. I suck his dick like I own it. Even when my arms fail me and start to tremble, I keep going. I can feel him about to come in my mouth, but Parker flips the tables on me once again.

He slaps my ass, hard. His erection pops free of my mouth, as I yelp. It happens so fast, one minute I'm straddling him, ass up, face down, sucking away. The next minute he's driving into me in one deliciously rough thrust.

I cry out, my back bowing, sending my breasts thrusting forward with a bounce. Feeling him inside me takes this all to a new level. They say to be careful what you ask for.

~B~

Parker

I've been having a pity party for one all day. It started with me drowning in memories of my fallen brothers. Then, my vision started to go in and out. Hours began to go by and I couldn't remember how so much time went by.

I wanted to go to Lakia hours ago, but I kept getting in my own way. Forgetting what I planned to do or not being able to see clearly. I still haven't told her about the extent of my disabilities. I haven't figured out how. I hate talking about it all out loud.

However, when she didn't run from me screaming after seeing my scars, I wanted nothing more than to claim her completely. She's mine, whether she knows it already or not. I have no questions about it.

I can still feel my spine tingling from her sucking my cock, like it's a prize-winner sucker at a fair. I was ready to come, but I needed to get inside of her, to feel her in every way. I just didn't know that meant entering her would be allowing her into my soul.

From the moment I slid into her wet warmth, I could feel the connection. Even now as I guide her hips over mine and pump up into her, I feel the stirring in my chest. I reach a hand up for her ponytail, tugging her head back.

My eyes search her face. She's stunning, riding my cock with a look of pure ecstasy in her cola brown orbs. Her lips are parted, allowing her sweet breath to fan back into my face. I inhale her, driven by the need to taste her wine flavored mouth.

"You're mine," I hiss out, thrusting up harder and harder.

"Yes," she whimpers, rocking me to the core.

My fingers bite into her hair and her hip. I can feel her dripping in between my legs. My balls are soaked with her essence. I lick my lips to search out the flavor that came from that same pussy that's drenching me. I groan when I find it. No longer able to hold back, I take her full swollen lips.

She cries my name into my mouth, but I swallow it. Needing more, I release her hair and shift our bodies until she's on all fours. Never once do I break our connection. My eyes remain on her ass jiggling around my stiff shaft. Her cries become louder, calling to something deep inside me.

"You like that," I bite out. "You're going to come for me again."

It's a command not a question. I plow through the rippling sensation her pussy is creating around my pulsing length. The foyer fills with her cries, and the slapping of my hips against her thick round ass. I splay my palm over her belly, feeling that fleshy skin.

"So damn sexy," I groan.

I roar with pleasure. I love a woman with curves and a real body I can hold onto. Thoughts of filling her belly hit me hard. A child made from love.

You love her.

Yes, I do. I think I've known that for a while now. This is just another way for me to express it. I pound into her from behind, as if each stroke can drill my love into her. When I feel her tense up, ready to explode all over me, I can't hold back any longer. Her first gush forces my seed from my body right into hers.

"Don't move," I breathe heavily. "I'll get us to the bedroom as soon as I catch my breath. Don't move an inch."

"Wasn't planning on it, soldier," she whispers sleepily.

~B~

Lakia

"It was a routine sweep. One minute we were all laughing and joking around, the next bullets were flying everywhere. Redding was with me after the first blast. He took a bullet to the leg, but we were together. It was the second blast that sent everything to complete shit.

"I was so amped I didn't know I was on fire. I was trying my best to locate your brother," he pauses to swallow hard. "Can't remember much else. Just waking up in the hospital, charred and fucked up in the head."

I close my eyes as the tears flow. I've been wanting so badly to know what happened out there. I wanted to know what my brother's last moments were like, but now that I know, it hurts so much more.

I bury my face into Parker's chest. His arms tighten around me. We're both silent at first, while I try to smother my sobs. I sob for Myles and for Parker. I still think he's holding back some, when it comes to the extent of his injuries.

So much is making sense. There are times when I've noticed him start to limp out of the blue. This man beneath me is so strong. He's been through so much, but acts as if he's not struggling with not only his recovery, but the losses he took that day.

"Baby," he says tightly, stroking my hair. "Maybe you should go back to your place. I'll come by tomorrow."

I lift my head to look down at him. I know my disappointment registers on my face. I thought we formed a bond tonight. I had no idea he would toss me out after. Rejection starts to form into rage. I open my mouth to tell him off, but the smirk on his face gives me pause.

"I love the way your eyes light up when you're pissed. It's like a bomb about to go off," he chuckles, lifting to take my mouth in a deep kiss. When he breaks the kiss, he runs his thumb over my lips. "I wasn't tossing you out of my bed. I was giving you an out. I'm not much good company at the moment. You're welcome to stay with me as long as you like if you can handle it."

I cup the side of his face. I feel so selfish. I'd come here for my own comfort, but I see how much he truly needs mine. I lean in to softly kiss his lips.

"When I lo—" he cuts my words off with a hard kiss.

"Nope, you won't say it before I do. My daddy once told me you don't deserve a woman that acknowledges her love for you, before you pledge yours. I know I don't deserve you, but I sure as hell plan to act like I do. I love you, been in love with you for some time now. I love your boy too," he says, with a gentle tone I've never heard him use before.

I lower my eyes and lashes. I already knew he loves Isaac. You can see it in the way he interacts with him. I know my son loves him as well. However, hearing him profess his love for me sends my mind racing and my heart pumping.

Parker lifts my chin. I can see he's ready to hear the words back. Somehow, I know they're the healing balm he needs to start to his full recovery. A recovery I'm sure won't be easy, but I'm here to love him through it.

"Because I love you, I'll be here even when you're not good company," I choke out. "I'm here for you, Jake."

"Shit, my name sounds good on your lips. I think we should see how it sounds in a high pitch," he teases, pouncing with a sexy rumble coming from his chest.

CHAPTER ELEVEN

Sour Roses

Lakia

I'm still sweaty from my workout. I spent an extra hour in the gym and another in the gun range. Something has been nagging me about the details Parker gave about that last day with my brother. I don't know what to think about the way I've been feeling. There's just something tugging that won't let go.

I roll my shoulders and step out of my car. I have the key in the door, stepping inside with the mail in my hand, when I feel someone at my back. I turn ready to defend myself, only to find a grinning Toni holding up a bouquet of flowers.

I glare at him. He begged off on Isaac yesterday for the hundredth time. I swear, I almost throat punch him for the hell of it. He turns up his smile, trying and failing to be charming. His charm failed on me a long time ago.

"You look gorgeous. I see you decided to do something about those extra pounds, like I told you. Nice," he purrs.

Asshole.

"Hey, Toni?" I say with a sugary sweet smile.

He leans in, his eyes dropping to my lips. I smile wider leaning into him. His eyes travel to my cleavage.

"Do you remember that time my brother told you he knew where to bury your body, where no one would find it and he'd be sure to get away with it?" I say seductively.

He frowns. "Yeah."

"You know, I asked him once just how he would do it. You know Myles was always detailed and thorough and I'm a real good listener," I wink at him.

"What the fuck is that supposed to mean?" he hisses at me.

"Nothing, just wanted you to know I'm working on a new book. Those details will come in handy," I shrug, playing up an innocent, saucy smile.

Toni's jaw ticks, his eyes rolling over me. He steps closer, invading my space. This time I'm ready for him. He has stepped over my threshold into my property.

Wrong move.

"Go shower and change. I'm taking you to dinner," he orders.

"The hell, you are," a voice booms behind Toni.

The same voice that's been sending shivers through my body night after night. Parker has a key to let himself in at night after Isaac goes to sleep. I think he has used it ever since I gave it to him.

Toni spins on his heels, his back stiffening. "What business is it of yours?" he snarls at Parker.

"If it involves my woman, it's my business," Parker says, his arms folded over his chest.

His muscles are bulging at the sleeves of his white t-shirt. Note, a short sleeve t-shirt. He stopped hiding his burns from me after that first night.

Toni snorts. *"Your* woman?"

"Never stuttered in my life," Parker says easily.

"Funny, I thought Kia and I had an understanding. She's not seeing anyone other than me," Toni seethes.

"I never agreed to that. In fact, I told you a number of times we're done," I say dryly.

Toni's head whips in my direction, his eyes blazing with rage and hatred. He tosses the roses to the ground. His fists balled at his sides.

"Make my fucking day and step towards her. I'll beat the fuck out of you and drag your ass around this house, screaming like the little bitch you are. Go ahead, try me," Parker says in a deadly warning.

"You and that mouth just bought you a world of pain. This is my city. You're about to learn that," Toni fumes.

"What's a city to a God? You want to try me, come on. Welcome to my world," Parker snorts.

"Uncle Parker," Isaac's voice rings out. "Daddy!"

Damn. I was looking forward to watching Parker kick Toni's ass. Shoot.

CHAPTER TWELVE

Pull Over

Parker

It's been a long day. I had an episode during my evening class. Dr. Winsor was right about having a TA and my notes on cards. I was able to play things cool and let Shelby take over the class.

This shit is starting to take a physical toll on me. Headaches are becoming more frequent. I'm starting to become fatigued. I spend most nights trying to bury myself in Lakia. She wraps me in a security I never knew I needed. It rejuvenates me just when I think I can't do it anymore.

The sound of an incoming call fills my truck. I grin when I see Lakia's name on the dash. She's right on time. Just when I need her most.

"Hey there, Baby Girl," I answer the line.

"Hey, Handsome. You sound tired," her sweet voice washes over me.

"Long day, just want to come home and pass out on the couch with you. You still plan to write tonight?"

"Actually, Isaac went to Mama's. I was hoping I could spend the night having a little one on one with my man," she purrs.

"I think that can be arranged," I chuckle.

"Look who's sounding more awake already," she giggles.

"A man that knows what he has at home has a right to get excited about it."

I flick on my blinker to turn the next block, not too far from the house. That's when the flashing lights come on behind me. I frown, there was nothing illegal about my turn and I've been doing the speed limit.

"Honey, everything okay?" Lakia asks with concern.

"Yeah, I'll see you in just a bit," I reply, ending the call before she can ask anything further.

I quickly dial Ryder. "Listen, I have a feeling some bullshit is about to go down. Patch into my Sync and stay on this line. Mute your phone," I bark the orders quickly as he answers the phone.

Moments later, the officer that pulled me over takes his time sauntering over to my truck. I'm pissed, but I bite back my anger. I get the feeling this isn't by far a routine traffic stop.

"License and registration," the officer demands gruffly.

"Would you mind telling me the problem officer?"

"License and registration," he repeats.

"Again, I'm going to ask what seems to be the problem?"

"Mr. Parker, you might want to hand over your license and registration," he growls.

My brows shoot up. "Now who says I'm Mr. Parker? I could be a friend or his family," I lower my voice, looking him in the eyes. "I want you to think about what you're willing to do for a friend, how much you're willing to lose."

Instead of addressing my words, he proceeds to call for back up. I shake my head. Toni just dragged his friend into a big fucking mistake. I know for a fact Ryder has the police chief on the line and he's probably listening in on every single word.

"Step from the vehicle, keep your hands where I can see them," he instructs, as another squad car pulls up.

"Only a coward sends his boys to do his work while he watches from an unmarked sedan," I nod my head in the direction of the car I spotted as I dialed Ryder to begin with.

"Only a coward comes into town and messes with another man's family," the officer snarls, now pointing his gun in my face.

I could take him, and the other two officers that have been dispatched, in the blink of an eye, but I step out of the vehicle and comply. I'm in cuffs the moment I step out. I remain in cuffs, face down on the ground for longer than I care to admit. It has to be about a half hour to forty-five minutes that goes by while these assholes bullshit around.

Toni joins in to shoot the breeze, clearly the other two cops on the scene aren't aware of the full situation, but they don't protest the crap that's going down. This shit probably would have gone on longer if not for Ryder. I hear the police commissioner personally bellowing through the dispatch line.

I look up to see the first officer pale. The smug look on Toni's face vanishes. I think it has just sunk in. It may be his city, but it's my world.

~B~

Lakia

I pace back and forth in the driveway. I want to go out and drive around, but something tells me to stay put and wait. Parker should've been home by now. I heard the sirens in the background, before he hung up. He hasn't answered any of my calls since.

I twist my fingers in my shirt nervously. I just know something isn't right. My heart stutters as headlights move up the street, I scramble out of the way when I recognize the truck to be Parker's. I hurry to the passenger door, after he pulls to the back of the driveway, tugging it open, I hop up into the truck.

There's a storm rolling over his face. I can tell in the tension in his body, he's pissed. I move to climb into his lap. His head drops into my breasts. Running my hands through his hair, I kiss the top of his head.

"What happened?" I whisper.

"Toni learned an important lesson," he rumbles. "I want you to be more careful from now on. He's taking things too far and he has no idea who he's dealing with. He's a spoiled child, that makes him dangerous."

"Oh, my God. He pulled you over," I gasp.

Parker shrugs. "He had some friends do his dirty work. I've been through worse. I'm sure a few unpaid suspensions will make them all second guess the action next time."

"That asshole, now he's messing with the one thing he does do for Isaac," I growl.

Parker's strong hands knead my back. "I'll help out. You don't have to worry about it," he lifts his head to kiss my chin.

"That's not the point. You're right he is such a child. I should've listened to my brother, he tried to warn me. I'm so hard headed," I huff.

"He's wasted enough of my night," he kisses my lips, his hands running under my dress. "I love how your skin feels beneath my palms."

I can feel him growing beneath me. My juices flood my panties from his slightest caress. I love his touch as much as he loves touching me.

"Pull into the garage. We're not making it inside," I moan against his lips.

"You never have to worry about me coming home," he rasps. "My heart will always find its way to you."

I melt into his chest, as he speaks to my unspoken fear. I needed those words more than he will ever know. Someday they will be words that I cling to.

CHAPTER THIRTEEN

We're Not Over

Lakia

My entire body is sore, but I'm not complaining. If the windows in Parker's truck could talk they'd be singing to the rafters. The man is an insatiable beast. I didn't think I could possibly take any more, but I was the one that straddled him this morning with a nice wake up call. I guess that means I'm no better than him.

A knock at the back door startles me. It leads right to the stairs of the garage apartment. I'm in the middle of washing my hair in the kitchen sink. I reach for a towel, wiping shampoo out of my eyes.

"Babe, did you forget your key?" I call, while patting my hair dry.

I open the door and the air shifts. I peek through the towel to see Toni glaring at me. He moves forward, backing me into the house, throwing me off guard.

"Son of a bitch," I grind out.

"Your little boyfriend cost my partner his fucking job," he fumes.

"*You* cost Vern his job, asshole," I toss back. "It should've been you."

"He had complaints against him already. They axed him. I only got probation," he rakes a hand through his hair looking crazy. "Fucking commissioner took your boyfriend's side. Wouldn't even hear us out."

"Well, next time you'll stop to think about the BS you pull," I shrug.

Toni moves quickly, crowding my space. "I did what I needed to do to protect my family," he bellows.

"Your family? You sound like a lunatic. You don't pay your son attention unless it benefits you or gets my attention. You and I have been over for—"

He backs me against the wall and slams his palm against it. "Stop saying that shit! We've never been over! We'll never be over," he yells in my face.

"If you don't get the fuck out of my face. You better go get some help, Toni. This ends today. You jump in my face like this again, it's going to be a problem," I say low and menacingly.

"What? You're going to get your boyfriend on me," he taunts.

"I'm quite sure the last time I watched, *Enough*, it wasn't the new boyfriend that fucked that psycho ex up," I lean into his face, showing him he's not the only crazy one in the room.

He licks his lips, backing off a little. He reaches up to touch the scar I left with that lamp so long ago. I nod at him.

"Don't push me, I have a son to think about," I warn.

"If I can't have you, no one can. Don't push me, Kia," he warns back.

"Make sure your insurance is paid," I fold my arms over my chest. "Do one good thing for our son."

"Bitch," he hisses.

I shrug. "Bet I won't be the dead bitch in the end, *Bitch,*" I toss back. "Remember, Toni, I've never made you a promise I didn't keep."

His nostrils flare, but he turns and takes his ass out of my house. I sag against the wall. That man is going to make me make good on my word. I know he is.

CHAPTER FOURTEEN

Something's Off

Parker

I'm no fool and I know my woman too well. She's been distracted the last few weeks. She's planning something and it's more than a book.

I don't like how quiet her ex has been. He's been off the radar since his suspension went into effect. I get the feeling I'm looking at two sides of the same coin.

Lakia's distraction stems from that asshole. I'm going to deal with his ass, as soon as I prove he's behind this distance I feel. I've given him this much of a pass, given the fact that he's Isaac's father.

I blink a few times. A curse rips from my lips. I've been stewing in my thought's while driving around. I'm starting to believe that stress is a trigger for me.

I pull the truck over and try the breathing exercises Dr. Winsor suggested. I rub my eyes, trying to focus. I still only have tunnel vision. I throw my head back against the seat.

I'm spiraling. I know I have somewhere I need to be. I look at the address programed in the GPS, but it doesn't give me a clue as to where I'm going or why. I tell myself to push through and just get there.

I shake my head and start off again. I drive carefully, relieved when I realize I'm coming up on my destination. I turn into a residential street. It's a cul de sac. The GPS leads me to the last house on the block. I pull into the driveway and cut the engine. My brows knit.

"Why are you here, Parker?" I quiz myself in frustration.

The moment the front door opens and the gorgeous woman and small boy come out, it hits me like a ton of bricks. My vision doesn't clear, but I know why I'm here.

"I'm here for them. My family. My woman and my boy," I mutter.

Sighing, I get out of the car. It's time I have a talk with Lakia. She needs to know what's going on with me. It's only right I tell her if I want to take this next step.

CHAPTER FIFTEEN

Best Friends

Lakia

Something is different about Parker today. I noticed it from the time he arrived at Mama's house. I wish I knew what I could do to make it better.

I bite my lip, as I watch him with my son. No matter what's going on with Parker, he never lets Isaac feel neglected. He has been running around the backyard with Isaac for a few hours now. At first, he called out encouragement to Isaac, while he tore through the yard, soon he was right out there with him.

I lean in the doorway out of their sight as they take a seat on the back steps. I know I shouldn't eavesdrop, but I can't seem to pull myself away. These are the two most important men in my life. I'd stop the world for the two of them.

"Hey, Uncle Parker," Isaac says thoughtfully.

"What's up, buddy," Parker replies.

"I was thinking. You love mommy and I know she loves you. Maybe you should be my daddy," Isaac says hesitantly, but it's apparent he has been thinking about this for a while.

"You know what? I think you're a very smart boy. I was thinking the same thing. What do you say? You think she'll have me?"

I'm stunned. I listen to the pause Isaac takes, as if he's thinking it over. I don't realize I'm holding my breath, until my baby speaks again.

"Well, you're nice to her, you cook and help clean the house, while she writes her books. You're my best friend, I don't see why not," Isaac finally responds.

My heart squeezes. My little boy is so sweet. I don't think I can become anymore choked up, until I hear Parker speak up again.

"Yeah, well, you're my best friend too. We'll have to see if your mama can handle how broken I truly am. If she'll have me, I want to make her my wife and you my son," Parker says, as if answering his own thoughts.

"You mean your vision and your memory?" Isaac asks.

There's a pregnant pause, my brows furrow. My mind moves slowly to string Isaac's comment together. It's his next reply to Parker that crashes right into me.

"So, you figured me out, huh?"

"Yeah, sometimes, when we're playing you forget things, and sometimes when we're doing puzzles you slow down when your vision stops working," Isaac says.

Wow! How the hell did I miss that? Or did I?

CHAPTER SIXTEEN

Be Honest

Parker

Lakia's making me nervous. She's been watching me closely all night. I feel like my skin is going to fall off if she watches me anymore closely. I peek over at her as we pull into the driveway.

She rode over to her mama's in her mama's car, so we rode back home together. Today was a good day. I had a revealing chat with Isaac. That kid only confirmed I'm moving towards the right thing. I'm not getting any younger. I want Lakia as my wife and I want to have more children. Calling Isaac my son will just be a bonus on top of that.

"I'll carry him inside," I say, as I open Lakia's door, before getting Isaac out of his booster seat.

I think I wore the poor little guy out today. He doesn't even flinch as I place him on my shoulder and carry him towards the house. I kiss his forehead as I walk, wishing him sweet dreams.

Lakia and I work together to get him into his Black Panther pajamas and into his bed. I remember when life was that simple for me. It seems like centuries ago now.

"What are you thinking about?" Lakia whispers, as we make our way into the living room.

"My childhood, things were so simple once," I smile down at her.

"Are things so complicated now?"

"I don't know about now, but they were once or twice along the way," I admit.

"Like when," she bats those pretty lashes at me.

I don't think she knows how beautiful she is. She wraps me around her finger without even trying. I now know the hole that was once in my heart was waiting for her to come and fill it.

"While my uncles were all in the military, my father had wanted to live the simple ranch life with my mother. After her death, things changed. I needed to get away and I ran right into the army," I begin to tell her.

"Uncle Wayne had hoped I'd join the Navy, but I wanted to rebel in every way. It was my decision, my choice. Today, I think it was the best decision I ever made. It's the decision that led me to you," I reach to tug her into my chest, before she can take a seat on the couch.

"Is that right?" she beams up at me.

"Yes, Ma'am. The army led me right to love," I smile at her.

"If you love me, be honest with me," she locks eyes with me, looking into my soul. "Tell me why they discharged you. It had to be something bad enough to keep you from performing. What aren't you telling me?"

With a sigh, I lift her, coaxing her legs around me. I walk over to her favorite spot in the house, the window seat. I sit with my back to the window, caressing hers.

"I had some damage to the nerves in my leg from the burns. They didn't think I'd recover from that, but what sealed things was the sporadic loss of my peripheral vision. It comes and goes with no warning. I also had brain trauma. I lose pieces of my memory from time to time," the words spill free, feeling like a weight being lifted.

She nods, eyes searching mine. "The glasses. It dawned on me you never wore glasses the few times I saw you in the past," she murmurs.

"They're supposed to help, but they haven't done much," I sigh in frustration.

"Were you having trouble today?"

"Yeah, I forgot where I was going and my vision went on the way to your mama's. I followed the GPS to figure out where I was headed," I admit.

"That's why you set all your destinations, even to the store down the road and back," she muses, understanding lighting up her eyes.

"I have a few things I do to adapt," I nod.

"Jake, Baby, none of that will keep me from loving you. I figured there was more. My son is just more observant than I am," she clamps her mouth shut.

I narrow my eyes and smile at her. "You were listening to our conversation?"

"Maybe," she bites her lip.

"How much did you hear?"

She makes the cutest face, wincing. "*Well*," she drags out. "I may have heard a lot more than you would have wanted me to."

"Marry me," I breathe.

A gasp leaves her lips, her bright eyes fill with tears. I take her lips in a gentle kiss. Her fingers lace into my hair and lock there.

"Marry me," I say against her lips. "I want to call you my wife and Isaac my son. I want you to give me more children. Marry me, Baby Girl."

"Yes," she says through her tears. "Yes."

I cup her face and devour her lips. I can taste the salt of her tears, mixed with the chocolates she had earlier at her mama's. I groan.

I'll get to kiss this woman for the rest of my life. I will savor her like this, until I'm old and grey and can't move to get my hands on her. Even then, she'll know that I love her with everything I am.

I swallow her small whimper. My hands are actually trembling, as I move them down her face, over her neck, still lower, until I grasp the sides of her ribs. Lakia lifts the blouse she's wearing over her head, tossing it aside. I unclasp her bra, discarding of it as she did her shirt.

I lift my arms as she tugs my t-shirt up. It hits the pile next. I take my time kissing her shoulders, running my hands up and down her back. She feels as soft as satin. My hands make another trip down, pushing her skirt from her hips. She stands, allowing the fabric to fall to the floor.

I lift to stand, toeing my boots from my feet. We both work to get my pants and boxers down my legs. I'm already rock hard from the thought of making her my wife.

"Come here."

She comes right to me. My arms going around her waist, lifting her back onto my mine. I sit once again, this time reaching between our bodies to toy with her button.

Her face buries in my neck, one of her palms splay the window behind me. I bring her to climax, once, twice, close to a third time, but she has other ideas. Cupping my face, she rocks her hips over my hard shaft coating it.

I groan as her slickness slides over me. I slide into her on the next pass, my hands cupping her face as she cups mine. We stare in each other's eyes and I'm so grateful for the ability to have this sight.

"If I lost my sight overnight, I would brag for years about the night I stared into the rays of the sun," I husk out, as she rides me so slow, it feels like I'm being tortured, but I wouldn't have it any other way.

"Jake, I love you," she whispers, on a moan.

"I love you too," I groan. "I love you more than you'll ever know."

She shivers. My name spilling from her lips. Both her hands press to the window behind me, her breasts push into my face. I pull a nipple into my mouth sucking and licking around it. I can feel her gush as I draw the tight bud deeper into my mouth.

"Yes," she gasps.

She rocks her hips in circles, then up and down again. I'm right with her, meeting her stroke for stroke. Neither of us in control, both sharing in the load. I move my arms to band around her back, holding her to my chest. Her head falls back, her tight curls spiraling out around her head like a crown. It's one of my favorite looks on her.

I claw my fingers across her back, knowing I'm not going to be able to hold on like this much longer. I push Lakia right to the edge, watching the beauty of her going over.

Standing, I switch our positions. I place her on the bench seat, lifting her legs onto my shoulders and clench her waist. I begin to increase the pace, hitting her spot over and over. Squeezing her legs together, I move them over one shoulder.

Her hands go over her head, pressing to the cool glass. I place one hand over hers and with the other I find my own purchase against the window. I drill into her, lifting her body from the bench.

I can see when she's about to lose it and start screaming. I cover her mouth with mine, but I don't let up. I slow again, when the slapping sound starts to ring through the room.

"Oh, my God," she whisper groans.

"You drive me crazy," I pant over her. "I can't get enough of you."

I feel her clench around me and groan. I pulse inside her. Our bodies having a conversation of their own.

"I think we both lost our minds," she giggles. "Maybe we should move this into the bedroom."

I shake my head. Damn, she's right. I shift her legs again, lifting her from the bench and start for the bedroom.

"Welcome home, Baby," she whispers in my ear as we enter the bedroom.

My soul falls at ease immediately. I know for the first time in a long time that I have a home. It's what I've been longing for. A home and a family. I have both now.

CHAPTER SEVENTEEN

Betrayed

Toni

I'm vibrating with anger as I watch this motherfucker carry my son into the house. That crazy bitch is really testing me. I'll be pushed but so far.

I sit fuming, waiting for this bastard to come back out of the house. I want to have a little talk with him this time. I've been in the mountains thinking, while waiting out my suspension.

I came back tonight with plans to talk some sense into Lakia, but then she pulls up with this asshole. I'm tired of playing games with her. This is bullshit and she knows it.

I wait, getting pissed when it takes too long for the asshole to come back out of the house. It doesn't take this long to get Isaac to his room and get the fuck out. He has crossed all types of lines with my family.

"What the fuck," I growl, when the fucker comes into view carrying my woman.

I grab the goggles to get a closer look. They sit in the window seat talking. My blood is boiling the longer she sits in his lap. I want to blow a hole right through the back of his head.

I watch her nod at something he has said. I wish I had more time to get the audio set up in her place. I can't hear a fucking thing and I don't have an angle to read their lips.

I watch some more, seeing him nod this time. I can see her biting her lip the way she used to do for me. I see nothing but red. I need to get closer. The right distance and angle and I can get audio and see their lips better.

I hop from the car looking around. I move into the shadows closer to the house, shoving the earpiece into my ear. I would have preferred to listen from the safety of the car, but this will have to do.

"*Well*," her sweet voice drags out. My heart squeezes to hear her talk to him so tenderly. "I may have heard a lot more than you would have wanted me to."

"Marry me," his voice comes through.

My blood boils. I'll kill him. I'll fucking kill him.

"Marry me," he repeats.

She better say no. I've played this game with her long enough. She better tell that motherfucker no and to get the fuck out.

He continues and I feel the vein in my head start to pound. "I want to call you my wife and Isaac my son. I want you to give me more children. Marry me, Baby Girl."

I shove my fist in my mouth to keep from roaring, but her next words drive me over the edge. I'm cut in half by the betrayal.

"Yes," she says. "Yes."

I can't tear my eyes away, as he cups my woman's face, devouring her lips. I shiver with rage, when I hear him groan. It hits me that he sounds like a man that knows the pussy before him well. I can't believe Lakia would give my pussy away. I taught her everything she knows.

I fade in and out as I continue to watch them undress each other like filthy animals. The grunting and moaning is disgusting. My son is in that house and she's going to just fuck this son of a bitch right in the front room.

Neither of them have thought of how sheer the curtains are. I swallow hard when her naked body comes into view. Lakia really has been working out. All of that chocolate skin is gorgeous on that body. It's been so long since I've fucked her, I can't believe she's about to open her legs to this nobody.

"Come here." His voice grates my nerves.

It kills me to watch her reach for him, but I have to be sure. I have to know if she really goes through with this. I'll forgive her if she walks away now. However, if she fucks him in that house with my son inside, we can never go back. I'm going to kill them all.

My jaw works as I see her hand press to the glass. The grunting and groaning continues to fuel my fury. A whimper rips from my lips as she tears out my heart. I know the moment she allows him into her body. His groan says it all.

The sappy shit that comes out of his mouth makes me sick, but her words. Her words are a sword through my chest.

"Jake, I love you," she whispers, moaning like a little whore.

"I love you too," he groans, pissing me the fuck off. "I love you more than you'll ever know."

When his name falls from her lips, while she rides him with a familiarity I can't stomach, my head feels like it explodes. Her hands press to the window again. Then that fucker sucks on the breasts that fed *my* son.

"Yes," she gasps, and I've had enough.

I tear the earpiece from my ear, but I stand there with my chest heaving, watching her give my shit away. I see the kind of whore she's become, allowing him to fuck her like a little slut.

"You're both dead, but she's going to suffer first," I seethe.

CHAPTER EIGHTEEN

...No One Can

Lakia

I've never been this happy in my life. Parker officially proposed about a week ago. It was adorable to see my big man so nervous. I guess it was with good reason. His memory failed him a few times, before it was all said and done.

It was heartbreaking to see his frustration, but I was patient with him and his little buddy was there to help. Isaac was so adorable giving Parker cues and clues.

We both decided on a small wedding, so Parker wouldn't be under that type of pressure again. I do believe it's stress that triggers things. I've gotten in the habit of running baths for him after work, so he can decompress. It seems to be helping a little.

In fact, I dropped Isaac off and I'm planning a romantic night that includes a long bath, dinner, and a movie. I sway my hips to the music, singing along.

Parker is on his way. He and Ryder went out for a bite. Ryder has some business he's been trying to get Parker to back. Apparently, Parker has some money stashed away. I haven't asked too much about that. I'm more than comfortable from my books.

I'm just curious about this business. Parker tends to blush whenever I bring it up. I have to say, Parker blushing is sexy. He has the whole Clark Kent thing down.

My phone rings, bringing a smile to my face. I turn down the music, entering my bedroom and flopping back onto the bed.

"Hey, girls," I chime into the phone.

"She lives," Dean sings out.

I laugh, "Whatever, even a small wedding takes time to plan and I'm raising a four-year-old," I sigh.

"Tell me about it," Kaye murmurs.

"Again, you heifers aren't about to sit on this phone complaining about in house dick. Shit, I can't wait to come to this wedding and see what's on the menu. I can't keep writing these sex scenes without an outlet," Dean grumbles.

Kaye and I burst into fits of laughter. Dean is crazy as hell. I love her though.

"What's up," I ask twirling a lock of hair around my finger.

I look at the lock and note I need to head in for a trim. Maybe I'll get a blowout for the wedding. I don't think I'll wear one of my lace fronts. Oh, I have to get Isaac fitted for the new suit. I think it's much cuter.

"I have a friend that could help end that book for you," Kaye whispers and I freeze.

I know what Kaye is talking about. I made a joke a few times over the years about hiring someone to make Toni disappear. I sit in silence, stunned at her words.

"Actually, a couple of friends that could give personal advice and solutions," Kaye says nervously.

I never told Parker about Toni's last visit, but I did share the details with my girls. I don't know what to say. I want to ask questions, but I know I shouldn't.

"I think I'm going to shelve that book for now," I say half-heartedly.

"Okay, but we're here if you need input," Kaye replies.

"I say write the fucker and be done, but whatever you want, hun. We want your mind free and clear for the wedding."

"Why do I feel like you guys have been talking about me," I burst out laughing.

"Pleading the fifth," Dean sings.

I hear a noise down the hall and look up at the clock. Parker must have been flying. I'm not expecting him this soon. I go to tell the girls I'll talk to them later, but something halts me.

"Girls, hold on a minute," I whisper. "I'm putting you on speaker. If you hear something funny, call the cops and Parker."

"Fuck them police, I'm calling Parker," Dean says.

I don't have time to protest. I hear another noise. I take the gun from the lockbox by my bed. When I enter the hallway, I place the phone on the little table.

With both hands free, I move up the hall. My heart is pounding. If it were Parker, he would have made his presence known by now. It's a habit of his. I want to hope that he just forgot to, but I have the feeling someone else is in my home.

I move stealthily trying not to make a sound. When I step into the kitchen, I skid to a stop. Vern is standing in the middle of the room looking like a confused slob. He runs a hand over his bald head.

"I shouldn't be here," he mutters.

"Then, why are you?" I snap. "Speak up, Vern, before I put a bullet in you."

I'm so damn pissed, I get ready to squeeze the trigger to teach his ass a lesson. I catch movement out the side of my eye, but it's too late. I feel the blow to the back of my head just before I blackout.

~B~

Parker

I still can't even believe I'm entertaining this harebrained idea Ryder has. Strip clubs. Male strip clubs. He and our crazy ass friends want to go out and shake their dicks at women, they can. They can count me and my money out. I can't even bring myself to say it in front of Lakia.

Shots.

I shake my head. Totally some Ryder shit. I think of Myles. He would have talked me into doing it. Hell, before Lakia, I might have. Now, I just don't think I want to get involved in that kind of thing.

My phone rings, causing my brows to knit when I see the name. Lakia gave me her friend Dean's number to pass to Ryder for wedding stuff. I don't know why she'd be calling this late.

"Hello," I answer feeling uneasy.

"Parker, Kia said she heard someone in the house. She told us to call you if we heard something off, there was a gunshot," she rushes out.

My blood runs cold. I step on the gas, without thinking any further. I have to get home.

"Thanks," I cut the call.

I'm already making the next call, as I race towards the house. I'm too far away. Two blocks would be too far I'm about five miles away.

"Did you change your mind that fast," Ryder answers.

"A gun went off at the house," I say without any emotion.

The soldier within has taken over. I have one mission and that's getting to my woman and getting her safe. I stay as calm as I would in the desert. I have to because there's no way I'm forgetting a damn thing right now.

Ryder doesn't even reply. The line goes dead. I already know he's on it. Before this night is over there will be one dead cop.

~B~

Lakia

I groan, but it seems to echo. It takes a third groan before I realize I'm not the only one groaning. I lift my lids and look around. I'm tied to a chair in the middle of my living room.

The groaning is coming from Vern, he's on the couch, bleeding all over my furniture. I knit my brows, confused. My head is throbbing.

"You shot me, Kia. The fuck," Vern groans when he sees my lids open.

I guess I did get that shot off. I smirk, glad I hit his ass. I know he's not here to talk tulips and roses. I feel no remorse.

"Shut the fuck up," I hear Toni hiss and turn to find him pacing.

He has on a bulletproof vest, his hair looks wild and his eyes are crazy. In this moment, I don't know what I ever saw in him. I lick my lips. I have to get out if this chair. I wiggle my wrists and wince when the cable ties dig into my flesh.

"Your job was to distract her and get the fucking gun. How the fuck do you get your ass shot," Toni spits. "This is all going to shit."

"You said it would be easy. Make it look like a break in and murder. You'd get the cash and the kid. You said she was a shit shot. She aimed right at my fucking leg and shot me," Vern groans.

"Quit your fucking whining. The boys have surrounded the place. I need to think, we need a way out of this," Toni panics.

"I didn't need this shit man. My wife is going to leave me. All I needed was some quick cash," Vern moans.

"I said shut the fuck up," Toni bellows, lifting his gun and putting a bullet in between Vern's eyes.

I jump. He's lost his mind. He was partners with Vern for years. Since he was a rookie. Vern was like a big brother to him. I close my eyes and say a prayer. I need to get out of this chair. I'm not the one dying here tonight. I need to get to my son.

~*B*~

Parker

Another shot goes off and I try to fly into the house. I fight against the officers, trying to hold me back. It takes Ryder, Doc, and Uncle Wayne to hold me back.

"Calm down, son. You flying in there isn't going to help anything," Uncle Wayne tries to sooth.

"Standing out here isn't doing shit either. What if he just shot her?" I say brokenly. "They've been sitting out here with their thumbs up their asses because he's one of their own."

"He's right, I'm tired of this shit. We need in there," Ryder growls.

Uncle Wayne nods. He inhales a deep breath. "You three get in there. I'll keep them busy out here," he lowers his voice, looking each of us in the eyes. "I have equipment in the back of the truck. Drive it around the block."

I'm in motion without a thanks. We've been waiting too long. Once they identified Toni and his partner as the suspects that entered the house, things seemed to start moving in slow motion. It's total bullshit and they know it.

We jump in Uncle Wayne's truck and suit up. Doc drives us around the block. I changed my routine to jogging in the neighborhood. I know which house backs up to my garage apartment.

We move swiftly, with me in the lead. I move on instinct, it all comes back to me, flooding my system. I feel like Myles is with me. He won't let me fail this mission. It's what I came here for, to keep Lakia safe. Myles always knew something was up with this lunatic.

I stop to get a look into the house. I can see straight through from the back door. Toni is just out of range, but I can see Lakia dead center, sitting in a chair she's been tied to. I tamp down my rage. We need to get her out.

I signal to Ryder and Doc, we need a shot. We could probably get one on the front side of the house through the window, but we need to stay out of sight. I curse under my breath.

If we enter, we'll have to engage him. I'm not comfortable with that. Lakia is too vulnerable. My head starts hurting through my frustration. I grind my teeth.

"I might be able to get a clean shot from the garage apartment," Doc's voice enters my earpiece.

"We need the bastard to move," Ryder growls.

Just then, as if feeling me willing her to, Lakia lifts her head in my direction. Her eyes meet mine and I see the trust there. She knows I'm here to get her out.

~B~

Lakia

I want to burst into tears when I see him. At first, I thought I was seeing things, but I know that man anywhere. I can read the look of frustration on his face. Immediately, I understand the problem.

After shooting Vern, Toni has been standing out of firing range of the windows and doors. It makes sense, as a cop he knows their next actions. Still, I need him where someone can take his ass out.

I would pick Myles' brain for scenario after scenario for my books. I mentally download all that information and look around the room. I know what I need to do. My hands and feet are useless, but my mouth still works.

"Did you even think about our son?" I say, drawing Toni's crazed eyes to me.

"Did *you* think about our son?" he snarls. "You fucked the piece of shit like a little whore, while my son was under the same roof!"

I swallow. I need to be careful. I need him to move, not fly off the handle and just shoot me in the head. I take a deep breath and try something new.

"Where did we go wrong, Toni? Why are we hurting each other?" I coo.

His eyes soften, he looks down at the floor as if he's lost. I see so many emotions cross his face. I think he's not going to answer at first.

"My father loved you. He said so from the first time I brought you to the house. I didn't think he would, but you wrapped him around your finger. He didn't care that you were Black. You were a good woman, he said.

"The more we dated the harder it became to please him. He wanted me to pull favors on the Force for his guys. I risked everything and did shit I thought I would never do. He still wasn't happy. When I got you pregnant, I thought he'd be happy. Instead, he pressured me the entire time to marry you. I knew you weren't ready. I needed to work you more.

"But he pushed, and I did it anyway. I proposed and you flat out told me, no," he lifts his eyes to glare at me. "My old man died a week later."

I groan internally, this is not helping. He hasn't moved and he only seems to be getting more pissed off. I did tell him no. He'd become more possessive and controlling. I refused to marry someone like that.

"We were going through so much. The pregnancy was so hard on me. I was tired," I say gently.

"I wanted to be there for you. I just didn't know how. My father treated me like shit when no one else was around. You thought he was such a good man. I never wanted to fuck Isaac up the way my father did me.

"You've always been too good for me, Baby. I just thought if I gave you space you would see how good things were between us, when they were good. I was giving you time to miss me," his eyes light up and his face becomes animated.

"I bought a house in the mountains. It's perfect, the dream kitchen you talked about. I built a jungle gym in the backyard for Isaac. It's been ready for a year now. I figured I'd show it to you after the new book. Then that fucker showed up," his face darkens again.

"He doesn't matter," I soothe. "Tell me about the house."

"Don't fucking lie to me," he bellows. "I saw you fuck him in the window for everyone to see. I heard you tell him you love him."

Fear ices over my veins. I know I've just found the final trigger. Toni sounds so lost and broken. I swallow hard, not knowing if I can get him back on the hinge. Just when I think all hope is lost, Toni drops to his knees and crawls to me.

He moves to position himself between my legs, wrapping his arms around my waist. He starts to sob like a broken child. Burying his face in my midsection. I don't move, I'm frozen as he falls apart.

A few moments pass, before I lift my eyes to see Parker and another shadow have entered the house during the distraction I provided, but they still need a clear shot. I need to get Toni away from me. I can feel the cool metal of his gun, and the one he took from me after knocking me out, pressed against my back. I lock eyes with Parker, instantly I feel like he sends me his strength.

"I did it all to make you jealous, Toni. I wanted you to give me and Isaac more of your attention. Remember how turned on I would get when you would get all jealous over me?" I purr.

It's true. When I was young and dumb I thought the way he would fly off the handle was sexy. Now I know better, the signs were surely there.

"Yeah, Baby," he nods, kissing my belly.

My skin feels like it's crawling, but I push through. "I see now that you weren't ignoring us. I'm so sorry. I should have been patient. You always told me I was so impatient," I keep talking.

"You are," he drops one gun and starts to caress my thigh. "I don't know if we can fix this, Kia. I fucked up. We'll have to run. We'll come back for Isaac."

"Okay," I whisper.

"Okay?" he lifts his head to look up into my eyes. His grey eyes shine with hope.

I feel so sorry for him in that moment. The man I used to know has shattered into pieces. This isn't even the confident guy I met in that college campus parking lot.

"Yes, okay," I nod.

"I knew you were the one. From that night I pulled you over. Do you remember that. It was raining, you and your friend were soaked through, but you were still beautiful. I followed you for weeks, before I let the air out of your tire in that parking lot," he smiles like a lunatic.

My brows furrow, my mind racing back all those years. Toni was a gorgeous cop, an older one at that. I'd been so flattered when he came to my rescue on campus, then asked me out to dinner.

I gasp when I remember the night he pulled me over. I'd been with Myles' ex-girlfriend. We went out to a party and she'd had too much to drink. I ended up driving us home in her car. Neither of us realized she had a broken tail light.

The officer was so polite and let us off with a warning. I was too nervous to look at him or take in any details. I was a young black girl, driving in a drunken white girl's Benz. I just wanted to get home.

Now, those eyes. I knew I'd seen them before when he pulled up in that parking lot. I was so young and stupid.

"I told you we'd be together. There was never any doubt that I'd hold on to you. If I can't have you no one—"

He doesn't get to finish. Parker puts a bullet through the side of his skull. Toni was too focused on me to see Parker and Ryder move into the room and find the right angle.

I just stare down at the body slumped in my lap. It's over, it's finally over. I've always known it would come to something like this. It was never my overactive imagination. I knew.

Ryder kicks Toni's body from my lap, as Parker cuts my hands free. Ryder cuts my feet loose just in time for Parker to lift me from the chair into his arms. He buries his face into my hair and holds me so tight, I think I might break.

"It's over," I whisper. "I'm free."

CHAPTER NINETEEN

You and I

Parker

I haven't wanted to let Lakia out of my sight. I know that motherfucker is long gone. I made sure of that, but the thought of how close I came to losing her. I just can't do it.

"I'm okay," Lakia says for the millionth time.

I grunt my acknowledgement, but I don't loosen my hold on her or unwrap my leg from around her. Ryder let us crash at his place, while he went to Miami with Doc for a few days.

Shots.

I still can't believe they're going through with that shit. Most of all, I can't believe I handed over a check for it. After they helped me get my woman out of that house, it was the least I could do.

"You can be a broody old bear. You know that," she giggles.

I look down at her. Those eyes sparkling up at me. I've never loved anyone more in my life. I don't know what I would've done if I lost her.

"I'm not going anywhere, Jake. If you hadn't come when you did, I was about to break out my Kung Fu style," she teases.

I growl at her and take her lips. I kiss her as if it's our last. When I pull away, her eyes are glazed over and she looks content with the world.

"I'm glad you can joke about it. I'm still too pissed," I gruff.

"He doesn't deserve another second of my life. He manipulated me for years. The best thing I got out of it all was Isaac."

"How do you want to handle this with him," I ask cautiously.

"It's Isaac, in time he will tell us what he thinks. I don't want to bring it up until I have to. Let him be a baby. He's happy, that's what matters," she shrugs.

"We can push the wedding back," I offer, knowing I don't want to wait.

"Like hell, we can. I'm not changing a thing. You get those rowdy friends of yours together and report for duty or it's going to be a fight," she sasses.

I burst into laughter. Rowdy, I guess that could be a word for my crew. I shake my head, tugging her warmth closer.

"We'll be there," I chuckle.

"Sooo," she drags out. "You ever plan on telling me what kind of business makes you blush every time it comes up?"

I groan, throwing an arm over my face. I knew this was going to come up sooner or later. I feel my cheeks heat just thinking about it.

"Ryder decided to open a chain of strip clubs and hire a bunch of vets," I peek under my arm at her.

"Aw, a bunch of super nerdy Veterinarians, that's hot. Are they going to have puppies too?" I roll my eyes at her, as hers light up with mischief.

"You know damn well what kind of Vets I'm talking about," I grumble at her, causing laughter to spill from her lips.

"Still, the puppies would be a nice touch," she giggles.

"I'll let Ryder know," I twist my lips at her.

Lakia nudges my leg off of her, moving to straddle my lap. I watch her cautiously. I know she's up to something. That pretty face always gives her away.

"Well, do I get a free show or two?" she purrs.

"Your ass will absolutely not be stepping foot in one of those clubs. You just forget we even own them," I huff.

"*We* own them?" A soft smile lights her face. "I'm going to be your wife, Parker. I'll always have the best view in the house. You don't have to worry. I was asking for a show from the sexiest of the owners."

"In that case," I lift and flip her onto her back. "Hands above your head. We have a no touching the merchandise policy around here."

She chuckles, but lifts her hands up, lacing her fingers together. I stare down at her naked body. I miss the extra pounds that have been melting away with her workouts, but if I have it my way, she'll be growing with my baby in her belly soon enough.

"Jake," she gasps, when I dip my head to suck her chocolate nipple into my mouth. "Please."

"Taking my time," I warn, chuckling when she huffs her frustration.

I kiss my way down her stomach, licking and tasting along the way. When I finally settle in front of her fat mound, I can see it dripping with her delicious honey. I take a moment to appreciate it all. Her thick thighs, her round ass, and the prize I'm about to devour.

She wiggles her hips, drawing my eyes back up her body. I love the little saucy smile I find. I give her ass a little slap, pulling a moan from her lips. She sucks her bottom lip into her mouth, her eyes glazing over with lust.

Sitting back, I flip her onto all fours. Running my hands up her back, I admire all that's mine. I massage her back for a few beats, building the anticipation. When I see her honey drip from her folds, my restraint breaks. I need a taste and I need it now.

I part her ass with my fingers and lower. Capturing the drip of her essence with my tongue, I drag through her folds all the way to her crack. Her pants and moans are like music.

I feast on her until my lips and tongue are numb and she's nothing more than goo on the bedsheets. I chuckle when she whimpers into the mattress. Reaching between my legs, I acknowledge the pulsing steel I've been neglecting.

Peeling her from the sheets, I turn her on her back. I groan and bite my lip, watching her breasts jiggle with the motion. I've never been turned on by a woman the way I'm turned on by the sight of her.

I lift her leg, kissing my way down her thigh, just needing to feel her skin against my lips. My hands caress anywhere I can touch. It's the simple touches that cause her to bow off the bed and give me looks that convey so much.

"You're everything to me," I whisper against her thigh, placing another kiss to her flesh.

"Show me," she demands.

I nod, moving between her legs. The moment I enter her I know things have changed again. I'm hers in a new way. The kind of love that's hidden deep and is found when needed most. When surface love just isn't enough, there's this love. The unbreakable kind that you have to dig deeper for.

"Don't give up on me, Kia. No matter what, don't let me go," I plead.

"Never," she whispers in my ear, as we climax together.

Precious Moments

Parker

I keep blinking. I want to remember this day for the rest of my life, but it would be great to be able to see it fully. I move my head to take in as much as I can. The things people take for granted.

Today I have to choose what's most important to see. My vision decided to fuck with me on one of the most important days of my life. I look away from the doctors, back at my wife.

Her face is drenched with sweat. She's still the most beautiful woman in the world to me. She's so brave and strong. I didn't know I could love her more than I already did.

I thought I was the luckiest man in the world when she said I do. Since that day, my life has only gotten better and better. Now this, my son is on his way into the world.

"Relax," Lakia whispers.

"I should be saying that to you," I frown.

"I'm familiar with the terrain. I got this," she winks.

I nod. "He's almost here," I say in awe.

She giggles at me. "You don't have to whisper, he's not going to change his mind and go back in," she teases.

"Mrs. Parker, we need one more good push," the doctor interrupts.

"Okay," she nods, licking her lips and bearing down. "Argh."

She lets out a little roar and the next sound I hear is the cry of my little boy. I turn my head quickly, not wanting to miss him and I swear it's like my vision opens up the moment I set eyes on him.

He's so small, but his cry is so big. He has entered this world making his presence known. I watch in wonder as they place him on Lakia's chest. They look perfect together.

"Should we name him Myles?" I ask, reaching to brush his little cheek.

Her brows knit. Slowly she shakes her head. When her cola eyes look up at me they seem perplexed.

"Mama always used to say, you don't name a boy after a man still living his legacy," she replies with conflict in her eyes.

My own brows draw in. I search her face for understanding. She bites her lip, I can tell she's debating whether or not she should say the words just on her lips.

"I had a dream about my brother. Mama never did feel like he was gone… For now, let's name our son something else," she says softly.

"Whatever you want, Baby Girl. You choose his name. I trust you," I wink at her.

ACKNOWLEDGMENTS

Hey!!! I bet this book was a surprise. I've been getting so many questions about this series and the funny thing is, each and every couple has an interesting back-story that can't or shouldn't be avoided. You need to know their beginnings to know how they get to the point of needing to be in that room with Caleb Perry. Which is way I've decided to do the novellas in addition to each full length. Some of these stories are going to tear your heart up, but it will be worth the journey.

Thank you so much, for your support and your patience. You see the way my brain is set up, LOL. These characters don't make it easy on me. I appreciate you all allowing them to tell their stories in their time and in their way. Again, your emails and posts are so appreciated. Thank you so much.

I love what I do and it allows me to get through so much. I thank those that understand my need to create and know how to let me do so. If I choose to write a story, it has a place. There's one person that knows of all the stories clamoring to get out and he just shakes he's head in wait. I thank him for listening to the crowded thoughts of my mind and not judging the stories that await. I'm grateful for the push to go and explore the voices that want to be heard.

Everything is working for your good. You have to trust the process. When people enter and leave your life, they all have a season, a reason, and some may be assigned for a lifetime. Don't rush any of it. Know what God has for you was planned even before you took your first breath. You are just going through the process of learning who you truly are. Their opinions never matter, their plotting will never prosper, stand in your favor and allow the Universe to guide the rest. Healing comes in faith. The faith to know it is done. You will have all that was meant for you. Be blessed in your portion. Thank you, Lord, for another one.

On to the Next!! *We're just one big happy family. Hahahahaha!*

ABOUT THE AUTHOR

Blue Saffire, award-winning, bestselling author of over thirty novels and novellas, writes with the intention to touch the heart and the mind.

Blue hooks, weaves, and loops multiple series, keeping you engaged in her worlds. Blue and her husband live in a house filled with laughter and creativity, in Long Island, NY. Yet, the city still calls to her to come on back for a visit.

Wait, there is more to come! You can stay updated with my latest releases, learn more about me the author, and be a part of contests by subscribing to my newsletter at www.BlueSaffire.com

If you enjoyed Broken Soldier, I'd love to hear your thoughts and please feel free to leave a review. And when you do, please let me know by emailing me TheBlueSaffire@gmail.com or leave a comment on Facebook https://www.facebook.com/BlueSaffireDiaries or Twitter @TheBlueSaffire

Other books by Blue Saffire
Placed in Best Read Order

Also available….

Legally Bound

Legally Bound 2: Against the Law

Legally Bound 3: His Law

Perfect for Me

Hush 1: Family Secrets

Coming Soon…

Other books from the Evei Lattimore Collection Books by Blue Saffire

Made in the USA
Columbia, SC
01 December 2020

26066344R00070